Falconer and the Great Beast

Also by Ian Morson

Falconer and the Great Beast

Ian Morson

St. Martin's Press
New York

Library of Congress Cataloging-in-Publication Data

Morson, Ian.
   Falconer and the Great Beast / Ian Morson.
      p.   cm.
   ISBN 0-312-20543-0
   1. Great Britain—History—Henry III, 1216-1272—Fiction.
I. Title.
PR6063.O799F345   1999
823'.914—dc21   99-14510
                                                                      CIP

First published in Great Britain by Victor Gollancz, an imprint of the Cassell Group

First U.S. Edition: July 1999

10 9 8 7 6 5 4 3 2 1

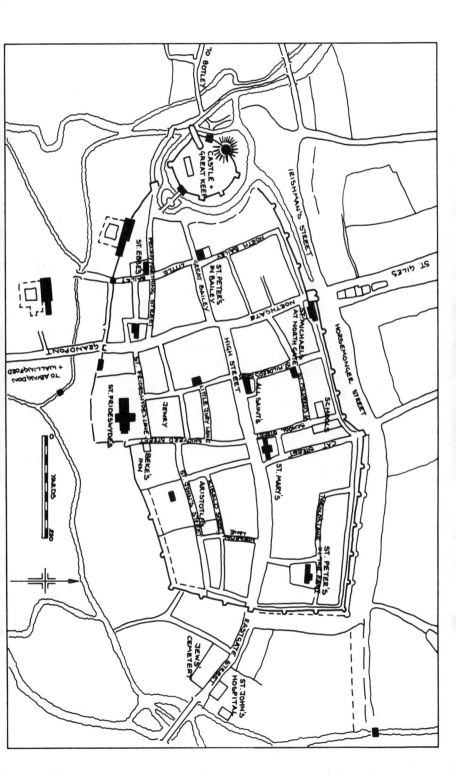

Prologue

These were the words of the Lord to me: Man, look towards Gog, the prince of Rosh, Meshech, and Tubal, in the land of Magog, and prophesy against him.

Ezekiel 38: 1–2

AD 1238

About this time an ambassador from Hungary came to the French king telling him that a monstrous and sadistic race of men had erupted from the northern mountains. They had lain waste to the lands west of the kingdoms of France and Germany, murdering all that stand before them. They have sent letters proclaiming that their chieftain is the messenger of God, and that he has been sent to subdue all nations. They are like the demons let loose from Tartarus itself, therefore they are known as Tartars. It is said the men have the heads of dogs, with sharp pointed teeth and flattened noses. Their eyes are pools of blackness and their countenances grim. They ravish and kill all before them, and devour all flesh raw, including human flesh. They drink the blood of their own horses in preference to wine. The women are chiefly admired for their ferocity and not for the womanly attributes of sweetness and compliance. They are very numerous and have been sent to be a plague on mankind. Some call them Magogoli – the sons of Magog – for they erupted from the mountains

where they had been incarcerated in history by Alexander the
Great. Nothing can prevent them from devastating the
countries of the West it seems.

From the anonymous *Chronica Osneiensis*

AD 1241

It is with sadness I have to report a most bloody battle on the
banks of the river Delpheos near the Danube. The Tartar chiefs,
with the houndish cannibals their followers numbered in a
thousand thousand, fell upon the combined forces of the Duke
Henry, the king of Bohemia, and the duke of Carinthia, together
with a detachment of Templars numbering nine brothers,
three knights, two sergeants and five hundred turcopoles.
They attacked on horseback, with clubs and swords, but chiefly
with bows – their greatest skill in battle. The armour on their
back is thin, so that they are not tempted to flee in battle.
When vanquished, they never ask for mercy, nor do they give
it. Against such odds, it was not long before the Frankish army
was defeated, and the flowers of chivalry lay dead upon the
battlefield. The Tartars fed upon the bodies in the field, leaving
nothing but bones for the vultures to pick over. I earnestly
plead with you sire to intercede with the kings of England and
France, for singly we will all be crushed by these barbarous
monsters.

Letter from Ponce d'Aubon, Grand Master of the
French Templars, to King Louis

AD 1249

'Tis said the Tartars are descended from the Ten Lost Tribes
of Israel, who abandoned the Laws of Moses and worshipped

the Golden Calf. They are thus the people who Alexander Magnus shut up in the Caspian mountains.

Letter from Frederick II, Holy Roman Emperor, to
Henry III of England

AD 1254

As the Son of Heaven, I scorn your feeble rebukes and question how you can claim to speak for God in these matters. Why should you find it strange that I have conquered the lands of the Hungarians and other Christians, since they have refused to accept the dominion of an empire ordained by God. I am the messenger of God on high, and you should know that no one can rule all the empires from sunrise to sunset except through the will of God. If you and all the kings of Christendom do not accept God's will and come to Karakorum to pay homage, then I will know you as my enemies.

Letter from the Great Khan to Pope Alexander IV

AD 1260

There rings in the ears of all a terrible trumpet of dire warning which, corroborated by the evidence of events, proclaims the wars of universal destruction wherewith the scourge of Heaven's wrath in the hands of the inhuman Tartars, erupting from the secret confines of Hell, oppresses and crushes the earth. Their law is lawlessness, their wrath is fury, and they are the rod of God's anger. If we cannot conjoin to defeat these fiends, the fate of nations will be that suffered already across the East, where old and ugly women are said to be eaten by the anthropophagi, and the beautiful ravished until they died of exhaustion, when their breasts are cut off to be dainties for their chiefs. I call to witness the faith in Christ, only by the power of which these Magogoli may be overwhelmed.

Papal bull issued by Alexander IV

AD 1263

At the same time, there came the most gratifying reports that the most potent monarch of the Tartars had, through the diligent teachings of a monk of the Black Order, converted to Christianity. The said king also sent consolatory messages to the French king urging and persuading him vigorously to wage war against the Saracens, and so to purify the whole land of the East. These letters, translated from the heathen tongue into Arabic and thence into Latin and French, also promised speedy and effectual assistance to be rendered by the Tartar king, as a faithful Catholic and baptized son of Christ. The French king was delighted and sent a small portable chapel, along with other precious relics, in the hands of some Preachers and Minorites whose task was to speed the spread of Christianity to the Tartars.

From the anonymous *Chronica Osneiensis*

AD 1268

Know that Chimbai is allied with Mangku-Temur of the Golden Horde in support of Kaidu. If they should strengthen their position in the East, then Kublay could be in danger. Abaka has empowered us to do all that we can to stifle this alliance. While the Mamluk, Baybars, occupies me in Syria, I must leave it in your hands to resolve the matter. I have hopes for this proposed alliance with the Frankish kings, so make sure that Chimbai does not return alive from England. I repeat in case the order is not clear enough for you – Chimbai must die.

Translation of an intercepted letter from the court of
Abaka, Khan of Persia

One

It filled the crossroads in the centre of Oxford with its bulk, and soon drew a milling crowd to wonder at its size. The skin was grey, thick and as creased as an old man who had spent his life toiling in the fields through scores of summers. A solemn man with the king's arms emblazoned on the front of his tabard stood at its head, holding a chain that looped around its enormous neck. Peasants in the crowd stood with their mouths agape, pointing calloused fingers at the monster. The black-clad masters of the university were equally agog, but outwardly behaved sagely, being more discreet in their examination, sharing whispered comments and knowing looks. A small child, bold in his ignorance, scuttled from under the protection of his mother's skirts, and slapped one of the tree-trunk legs that the beast had firmly planted on the ground. The woman shrieked, and made a grab for her errant child, pulling him away from the monster before it could breathe fire over her offspring, or rend him apart with needle-sharp teeth. But she need not have feared. The child's slap was nothing more than a pin-prick to the hide of the great beast, and the boy was retrieved without him being burned, eaten or crushed under the beast's great weight. The enormous ears, like vast wings, flapped back and forth, and the beast's head swayed rhythmically from side to side as though it was listening to some piper's tune in its head and unheard by anyone else.

Emboldened by the child's actions and seeing him come to no harm, the crowd pressed ever closer, pointing and gesturing at this great beast that had just arrived in the town. The people in the front of the press seemed oblivious even to the long curved horns that protruded from the beast's jaw, and the long proboscis that dangled down between those yellowy protuberances. Then suddenly the knot of students who stood at the head of the beast became too bold. One student, the worse for drink, it has to be said, made a grab at one curved horn. Another drew a short dagger, and began to prod the end of the questing proboscis. The ear-splitting squeal that resulted seemed to throw the whole crowd back with its force. Later, some in the crowd likened it to the final trumpet of Judgement Day, and for that one foolish, dagger-wielding student it very nearly was.

The beast tossed its head, and the man who had held it under control with the long chain looped around its neck lost his grip. To the crowd's astonishment, the formerly placid, earth-bound beast reared up and swung its head in pain. The youth who had stabbed at its tender trunk was struck by one of the graceful horns, the tip of which ripped through his leather jerkin, and tore the woollen shirt and pale flesh that lay beneath. The youth was thrown backwards into the retreating crowd, and landed in the dust, still and pale. The king's man, who until then had had control of the beast, recovered himself and scurried fearlessly between its legs, snatching at the swinging chain. Once he had a grip of the chain, he pulled on it, and cried out in a guttural tone that the beast seemed to understand. As quick to be calmed as it had been roused, the beast once more stood still, but now its massive eyes betrayed a fearful look that it cast wildly on its erstwhile tormentors.

Two students grabbed their fallen comrade, and lifted him up between them. He groaned, and the crowd gave a communal sigh of relief at this sign of life. He was conveyed away between the two youths, groaning and dripping blood in the dust. With the victim out of sight, a semblance of good humour returned to the crowd. But they now treated the great beast with more respect, eyeing it from a safe distance, while showing no sign of dispersing. Presently a bent-backed but muscular old man elbowed his way through the crowd, and spoke briefly with the beast's keeper. The king's man nodded curtly, and the sturdy old man pushed back through the crowd, shouting and waving his arms for the people to get out of his way. The king's man yanked the beast's chain, gave another guttural command, and the beast and its keeper followed the lurching gait of Peter Bullock, Constable to the City of Oxford, through the parting mob.

The arrival of the king's elephant in Oxford should have been wonder enough for that summer's day in the fifty-second year of the felicitous reign of King Henry III, but there was still more to marvel at that year in the university city. Peter Bullock had already been advised of another arrival expected in Oxford that day or soon after. And as dusk fell, and his watchmen locked the city gates, he paced the top of the new city walls, peering over the battlements. The meadow below the walls was dotted with bright flowers – the white constellations of daisies, red clusters of clover, and the yellow spikes of agrimony close to the wood's edge, where the trampling of students' feet had left the flowers undisturbed. But the sweetness of their presence left Bullock unmoved – his nose was more attuned to the stink of the ramshackle houses that lined St Giles outside North Gate, and Grandpont in the south. Oxford was bursting at its seams, and the poor and the whores now lived mainly outside the protection of its walls. They would have no protection from Gog and Magog.

The day had been long and hot, but now he could feel the chill of evening creeping into his bones. Or perhaps it was just the thought of what was approaching out there in the darkness. An old soldier never lost that sense of foreboding, which often came like a premonition of doom before a battle. He felt it now, and the hairs on the nape of his neck prickled. If they were out there, what's to say they wouldn't attack in the dark, as they had been reported to have done time and again all across the kingdoms of the West? That they were supposed to be here for a peaceful purpose could only be trickery in Bullock's eyes. His gnarled hand clenched tight over the pommel of his battered sword, and he strained to see into the growing darkness. There was nothing.

But with his senses heightened, he thought he heard the faintest sound behind him. The whisper of cloth against stone, perhaps. And before he could turn, a pair of strong hands held him in a vice-like grip. He struggled briefly, but it was no use – he could not draw his sword. He hoped his end would be a quick one.

'You're not as swift as you used to be.'

He heard laughter in the voice, and recognized it straight away. Recovering his equilibrium, he gruffly riposted, 'And you are not as silent as you were – I heard your robe brush against the parapet.'

The other man released him, and Bullock turned to confront the smiling face of William Falconer, Regent Master of the University of Oxford. The big man's hair was grizzled but abundant, unlike the constable's thinning white locks, his visage was lined but the flesh was firm and the jaw square. His most striking features were his piercing blue eyes that seemed to bore into the constable's very soul. And the memory of his strong and unbreakable grip reminded him of Falconer's strength. He wished his old friend hadn't crept up on him so, for it only served to remind him of his advancing years and failing powers. To cover his shame, he leaned over the parapet and looked out into the gloom. He heard the regent master move to his side, but didn't look at him.

'What's out there, that so draws your attention, Peter?'

Bullock strove to shock his friend. 'Gog and Magog.'

Falconer merely snorted in amusement. 'Gog and Magog! You know that, strictly speaking, Magog is a place, and Gog its prince. It's in Ezekiel – "Gog, the prince of Rosh, Mesheck, and Tubal, in the land of Magog". They are not two people.'

'I did not think I would ever hear you quoting the Bible at me,' Bullock mocked, but stubbornly pursued his tale. 'All right, they are not two people – but they are a horde.'

Falconer sighed in comprehension. 'Ahh. You mean the Tartars from the East. Surely they have not yet invaded England, let alone the vicinity of Oxford. So, look as you might into the darkness, you are unlikely to see this particular Gog.'

Bullock smirked in satisfaction. 'For once you are wrong, Regent Master. I have been advised by the sheriff that we are to expect a Tartar ambassador and his entourage. The message was brought by fast horse, and the party is close behind, so they will be here in the next day or two. They have been sent to Oxford to waylay the king, who is at present waging war on Llewellyn at Shrewsbury. Myself, I think the king is wise to avoid the ambassador at all costs.'

Falconer marvelled at this firm statement of the constable's viewpoint on regal affairs. He normally had little time for the politics of church or state. 'Why's that, old friend?'

'Because they're evil – Alexander Magnus was wise to seal them up behind the iron gates. Look what they've done to Christendom since escaping.'

'And to the Muhammadans,' Falconer reminded him, thinking it would at least make sense for the king to use the Tartars to overcome the Saracen threat to the Holy Land.

Bullock was not to be convinced. Squinting into the inky blackness that now enveloped the plain on the north side of the city, he was sure he could detect some movement. Peer as he might, however, he could detect nothing for sure. Anyway, if they arrived this late, the Tartars might hammer on the doors of North Gate till the Final Judgement, but he would not let them in. Even so, there pressed on his heart a feeling of doom as heavy and dark as the countryside beyond the walls on which he and his friend stood. Something terrible was going to happen soon.

Two

On that day, when at length Gog comes . . . the fish in the sea and the birds in the air, the wild animals and all reptiles that move on the ground, all mankind on the face of the earth, all shall be shaken before me. Mountains shall be torn up, the terraced hills collapse, and every wall crash to the ground.

Ezekiel 38: 18–20

The early morning sun, filtering into Falconer's solar at the top of Aristotle's Hall, found the regent master slumped over the heavy, scarred table in the centre of the room. Scattered around on its surface was a jumble of aromatic jars, some with their lids discarded and the scent escaping, and an array of animal bones. Chief amongst the remains was the skeleton of a large bird, the bones cunningly held together with sinew. The skeleton was laid out as though the bird, while alive, had been gliding through the air. On the floor underneath the table was a heap of reddish wing feathers, which, if they came from the same source as the bones, identified the bird as a kite. The feathers were not there as writing implements, for each had been pulled apart and closely studied, before being thrown on the growing heap under the table. Creating the means for a man to be able to fly like a bird was an obsession that occupied every spare moment that Falconer had.

But another matter had distracted him the previous night, and had occasioned a different sort of nocturnal research. Near his stiff and outstretched right arm lay a sheaf of papers that, before his conversation with Peter Bullock on the battlements of Oxford's city walls, had slipped out of his memory. Now the constable's dire warning had reminded him of their existence. Returning to the hall, where he presided over the education of a dozen students, he had retired immediately to his solar and the company of Balthazar. Balthazar was a barn owl that Falconer had tamed as a chick, which had now grown into a splendid, ghostly white bird. During the day the owl slept, as still as a statue, in a corner of Falconer's solar at the top of the house. Occasionally it would open its round deeply knowing eyes to observe its human companion, then return to sleep. Awake, it never proffered any opinion on Falconer's activity, and that's why he liked the sagacious bird. Oxford was too full of people ready to offer their opinion unasked. At night it stirred itself, and flitted silently out of the window in search of food, its easy flight mocking Falconer's stumbling efforts to copy it.

Last night Falconer had begun digging through the pile of books stacked next to his bed. Observing his master's preoccupation, the bird hopped to the open window, spread its wings, and flew off to quarter the meadows for mice. It had taken Falconer some while to find what he had been looking for, because he had long ago discarded it as a mere curiosity. Finally he remembered tucking the papers into the back of a copy of Priscian's *Grammar* – a book he rarely had recourse to. At the bottom of the stack of books he had accumulated since his arrival in Oxford many years before, he eventually laid his hands on the simple grammar book. Sure enough, there were the papers he was seeking, poking out from inside the back cover. He unfolded the stiff, resisting parchment and began to read the contents with a fresh eye.

The text was entitled *Epistola Alexandri Macedonis ad Aristote-*

lem magistrum suum de itinere suo et de situ Indiae, and purported to be a letter from Alexander the Great to Aristotle. Describing the nature of the countryside beyond the boundaries of the East, and the beasts that roamed it, it was relied on by travellers to inform them of what they might encounter when they ventured further than civilized man had done so far. Falconer's eyelids drooped as he read by the flickering light of a tallow candle about striped tigers, white lions as large as bulls, and bats as large as pigeons. He was disappointed, but not surprised, to find no reference in the letter to the Tartar race – he had always thought the letter a fake anyway. His head slumped over the parchment and he drifted into sleep, only to have his dreams inhabited by the beasts conjured up in the text. He found himself in a fantasy-land of massive trees and thigh-high grass that impeded his flight as he ran from the terrible odontotyrannus – a beast described as being as large as the elephant he had seen at Carfax that morning. But this beast had the black head of a horse, the sharp teeth of a wolf, and a vicious triple horn sprouting from its forehead. He ran and ran, but the beast gained on him as he fought to push through the clinging grass. He turned his head to look over his shoulder, and felt the foetid breath of the odontotyrannus on his cheek. He stumbled and fell, crying out as the sharp, cruel horns gored his shoulder-blades.

'Master.'

Falconer woke from the nightmare to find the bright sunlight of a new morning penetrating his vision. He unthinkingly lifted his head from the cushion of his left arm, and winced as a bolt of pain shot down his stiffened neck. He could hardly move his outstretched right arm at all, and the fingers were without feeling. Cautiously, he turned his head to look at whoever had been tapping his shoulder. His screwed-up eyes discerned the features of Richard Bayley, a fresh-faced youth from Isleworth, who was soon to complete his first year at the university. Richard had not succumbed to the world-weariness that characterized most of his companions, and his face would usually be relied on to be staring up in wonder as Falconer gave his lectures in logic. This morning, his pink and beardless visage was more than usually animated. Falconer eased himself upright and pins and needles lanced down his numb right arm.

'What is it, Richard, that gets you up so early? And gives you cause to disturb my slumbers.'

The youth was immune to the mild rebuke in Falconer's words, and he grabbed his master's arm.

'Come. You must see. They're camped on the fields outside North Gate.'

Falconer was about to enquire who 'they' were, when he remembered Bullock's words about the Tartar ambassador and his impending arrival. Was it truly he who had arrived, and would he and his entourage resemble the beasts chroniclers described them as? He stirred his aching limbs and followed Richard Bayley down into the streets of Oxford. Balthazar, his belly full, was back on his perch, oblivious to the wilder imaginings of men.

Chimbai donned his raw silk undershirt and stuffed it into the waistband of his heavy grey trousers. On top of the shirt he pulled on his blue tunic, the kalat, which was decorated with gold thread at the cuffs to denote his standing. His rank was that of noyan, above which there was only the rank of tribal leader, or khan. Finally, though the sun shone and the sky was clear outside the yurt, he placed a cone-shaped cap on his head. This cap was fur-lined and had a curved design that showed he was of the ancient Khorilar clan. Chimbai could claim a common descent from the ancestors of the great

Chinghis Khan, and that ancestry was reflected in his swagger-ing walk as he crossed from his main yurt to the tent in which he kept his images of the great god Tengri.

The sun was bright, but the air was heavy with a dampness that Chimbai found irritating, for it filled his chest with a heavy humour. He yearned for the dryness of the winter plains where his forefathers had pastured their cattle. This infernal little island they had landed on a few days before was claustrophobic, and damp. He would carry out his task as quickly as possible and return to Comania as fast as his horses could bear him. He had already sent the Christian priest into the city to find the English king's envoy, who, he had been promised in London, would be awaiting him. He cast a practised eye over his personal guards, who encircled his private tent, rendering it out of bounds to all who travelled with him. The three men were alert and well-armed, and knew better than to let him down – their very lives depended on their obedience to his orders. Just as he was about to enter the yurt, he heard someone call his name. Glancing over to the entrance to the second large yurt, he saw the stocky figure of his deputy, Guchuluk, striding towards him. Quite deliber-ately, he chose to ignore the younger man, and stepped into the small yurt, dropping the heavy flap behind him. He relished the thought of Guchuluk being humiliated by the men of his ten-troop *arban*. He was hot-headed enough to try to get past them to say whatever it was he wanted to Chimbai, and they would be implacable in denying him access to their commander. The youth never learned his lesson.

The yurt was in semi-darkness, a narrow shaft of light spearing down from the small opening in the apex of the tent. Chimbai removed his fur-lined cap and stepped towards two figures that occupied the rear of the yurt. He bent down reverently before them and picked up a wooden bowl at their feet. Dipping his fingers into the greyish animal fat in the bowl, he transferred some of it to the mouth of each figure, smearing it across the crude representation of their lips. Next he took up a skin which was full of water, and dribbled the contents on to the greasy visages. Having shared his bounty with his gods, he stepped back, and, standing with his feet firmly planted on the ground, he raised both arms in salutation. He uttered the prayer he had learned as a child, then stood motionless. As was his invariable habit every morning, he maintained this uncomfortable pose for a considerable time, silently worshipping the spirits of his ancestors.

When Falconer reached the battlements of the city walls, he found Peter Bullock in more or less the same spot as he had left him the previous night. But now he had been joined by twenty or thirty townsfolk, who all gazed nervously over the crenellated wall. Richard Bayley, who with his young legs had beaten his master to this vantage point, pointed eagerly over the wall.

On the fields that lay immediately beyond Candich, which encircled the city walls, was a sight to outdo the strangeness of the great beast that the citizenry of Oxford had revelled in the previous day. In the middle of the grassy sward that usually witnessed the energetic physical pursuits of the students of the great university, an encampment had sprung up overnight. But it was an encampment the like of which even William Falconer on his travels had not witnessed before. Three circular, black structures, each topped with a shallow dome, had grown out of the parched earth, two larger than the third. The flowers that had sprung up despite the dryness of the summer were now trampled underfoot. From one of the two larger tents, there rose a lazy plume of smoke that drifted into the summer sky. To Falconer, the scene was blurred and unclear, and he delved in the pouch at his waist. From it he drew a v-shaped device with glass set in rings at the extremity of each arm. He held this device to his face and peered through the lenses. The view below him came into focus. Though he gave his students the impression that his pale blue eyes could search out the slightest misdemeanour deep in their soul, his vision was weakened by years of studying close and poorly drafted texts. These lenses, devised by a Jew of his acquaintance, remedied the weakness.

Still he could see nothing stirring in the encampment save the livestock. Beneath the trees that edged the field was a group of six or seven corralled horses unlike any Falconer had seen. They were thickset, with short legs, and their skulls had a broad, bony forehead. They stirred restlessly as though impatient at being confined, raising clouds of dry dust from their agitated hooves.

'Is that them?' enquired the ingenuous student at Falconer's elbow.

'Who?' Falconer was puzzled by Richard Bayley's question.

'The Tartars – I have heard they have the head of a man but the body of a horse.'

Falconer guffawed at such credulity. 'And others say they are dog-headed cannibals. Beware of any hound you see in the street – they might be Tartars, come in the night to consume you.'

The youth paled at the thought, not recognizing it as a jibe, and glanced nervously at a dog that foraged in yesterday's market litter in the lane below. One of the townsfolk who stood close by must have heard Falconer's jocular remark too, for a whispered thread of horror ran through those who stood on the battlements with Falconer. He was about to disabuse them of their fears when Bullock muttered under his breath:

'Here they are.'

Falconer quickly raised the lenses to his eyes again and looked at the entrance to one of the larger tents. Three short, stocky men emerged, and hurried over towards the nearby smaller tent, where they arrayed themselves around it in a protective circle. They were all dressed in the same long blue tunic with red edging at the cuffs and collar, over which they wore a short jerkin of leather strips. Each had a short scabbard at his waist, a curved bow, and a quiver of arrows.

Falconer felt someone nudge his arm. It was Peter Bullock motioning him to look back at the tent flap from which the three men had come. From it emerged another stocky figure, but this man was much more imposing than the three before him. His tunic was edged in gold, his cap fur-edged and outlandish, and his manner was self-assured. He stood before the entrance to the tent, his feet planted wide, as he surveyed the world. The early rays of the sun lit up his impassive, leathery face, and Falconer didn't know whether he was aware of the crowd observing him or not. He felt sure, however, that the man cared little if he was being gawped at or not. The look on his face as he stood before his tent was that of a man who reckoned he owned everything he set his eyes upon – and nothing, or nobody, would stand in his way.

The Tartar strode over to the small tent and entered it, ignoring the call of another person who had emerged from the second of the large tents. This man, younger and less imposing, strode over to the tent where the older man had disappeared, only to be stopped by one of the three guards. Despite an angry exchange of words, that drifted up like guttural barks to the top of the city walls, the second man was turned back, a livid look on his tanned features. He stalked back to his own tent and disappeared inside.

For a while nothing further occurred on the playing fields that had been usurped as the Tartar encampment, and the crowd that had gathered on the city walls began to disperse, leaving Falconer and Peter Bullock to debate the tableau that had been enacted before their eyes that sunny morning. Bullock spoke up first:

'Not all rosy in the Tartar camp, then.'

Falconer just grunted in agreement. He had never supposed that this implacable war machine was made up of anything more than human creatures the same as those in the West. And if that were so, they were prey to the animosities and rivalries that everyone experienced. As if reading his mind, Bullock posed a question for him:

'Talking of disagreements between men, have you seen Humphrey Segrim lately?'

Cautious of what might lie behind his friend's words, Falconer responded with a question of his own. 'Why? Should I have?'

The constable pursed his lips. A person of epicurean tastes, he would be the last to condemn a man for making a fool of himself over a woman. He had pleasured himself with plenty a lusty maiden in his time, and had avoided the snares of wedlock in the process. But therein lay the problem for his friend. The woman he pursued was married, and her husband still alive. Indeed, the fact that he was alive was due in no small part to the quick thinking of the very man who now paid court to his wife behind his back. Regent Master William Falconer had pummelled him back into existence after an errant priest had all but squeezed the life out of him. That the marriage of Humphrey and Ann Segrim appeared to be a sham as far as the bedroom went was no reason for a supposedly celibate regent master to jeopardize his position at the university. Especially when the whores of Beaumont could provide a most satisfactory service to a man in need of comfort. The constable couldn't understand his friend's apparent desire to ruin himself, even though he had to admit that Ann Segrim was some beauty. He could relish ruining himself over her in any other circumstance. He knew Segrim's suspicions had been aroused by his wife's regular trips to Oxford from their estates at Botley, and had urged Falconer to deny the rumours to Segrim's face.

Falconer was about to explain that his relationship with Ann Segrim was purely one of master and student when he spotted something happening in the camp, and raised his eye-lenses to his face once more. Suddenly his face paled, and with a muttered expression of disbelief on his lips, he fled down the stone steps and along the lane towards North Gate.

Three

These are the words of the Lord God: In that day when my people Israel is living undisturbed, will you not awake and come with many nations from your home in the far recesses of the north, all riding on horses, a great host, a mighty army . . . and in those future days you will be like a cloud covering the earth.

Ezekiel 38: 14–16

T he Franciscan friar stooped as he brushed under the flap of the greased felt tent his Tartar hosts called a yurt. The morning was bright and clear, and the walls of Oxford stood before him. He took a deep breath and caught the scent of the summer flowers growing in the meadow. It had been so long since he had stood and smelled the flowers in England. For a moment he felt almost giddy with excitement.

He had met the Tartar commander and his entourage at the port of Calais as they waited for a storm to subside and a sea crossing to become possible. He had travelled from Paris, and he, too, sought to cross the Channel. Forced by the teeming rain into reluctant proximity with these strange people with outlandish clothes and even more unusual facial features, he listened in to their conversation. Unfortunately he understood not a word. The guttural tongue that they shared was like nothing he had heard before. And, shut away as he had been for the last ten years, he wasn't even certain where they came from. Little news had penetrated the monastery in which he had been incarcerated, and what had was carefully screened from him. Now this new pope had seen fit to persuade his order to release him from his confinement, and to encourage him to write down all his accumulated knowledge. It didn't extend to these strange men. In fact, he was only just beginning to discover how the world had turned since he had been obliged to leave it all those years ago.

Then it suddenly struck him, were these the fiends from Hell that Christendom had so feared when he had been in the world still? Could things have changed so much in ten years that the terrifying Tartars, who had been devastating Christendom, could now be merely peculiarly garbed strangers to gawp at? Humble fellow travellers? If they were Tartars, then things had changed indeed! He suddenly felt deeply angry at being deprived of human intercourse for so long, and it made him feel old. One of his favourite prescriptions for keeping mentally young came to mind – *listen to beautiful music, look at beautiful things, hold stimulating conversations with sympathetic friends, wear your best clothes, and talk to pretty girls.* He had been allowed none of these for ten years, and he had missed the casual gathering of information that they afforded any human being. Now, despite his difficulty in mingling with people again, he was anxious to learn what had been happening since his incarceration, and decided these strangers would make interesting travelling companions.

He could tell the motley group viewed the prospect of travel on a ship with trepidation, and it amused him to compare this reality with the concept of the devilish Tartar horde that had so terrified the civilized nations in the West. He wished King Louis of France could have seen the fear in their eyes at the prospect of trusting to the small English barque that tossed on the pounding waves close to the quayside. The dock was piled high with their baggage train, and a herd of skittish but sturdy horses milled around in a temporary corral. But, despite their own fearfulness, the Tartars obviously still instilled fear in other people. The sailors who frequented the port, a hardy breed of men normally, were giving the stony-faced soldiers a wide berth. One or two even resorted to gestures which the friar recognized as signs to ward off the evil eye.

As the rain bore inexorably down, the friar eyed the group closely. He saw that one of the men wore a Christian cross on a chain around his neck. Boldly crossing over to him, he addressed him with a greeting in Latin. The man's face broke into a smile, and he spoke back haltingly in the same tongue. The friar found it difficult to understand the accented speech, until the other man suddenly spoke in English. Once over his initial surprise, the friar responded, and the two were soon deep in conversation. The Franciscan learned the man was a Nestorian priest from beyond Comania by the name of David. This name had surprised the friar a little, for though the man professed a Christian faith, albeit one deemed heretical by the Roman hierarchy, he was of the same race as the soldiers. Those same soldiers were already eyeing the two priests' conversation with suspicion. They were all short and stocky, with veiled, slanting eyes. Some were clean-shaven, and some sported wispy black moustaches. Most had fearsome scars slashed across their cheeks.

With his imperfect English, David still managed to explain that many of his tribe were Christians, as were some of the royal house of the Great Khan, Kublay. And he had been given a Christian name at birth. But before he could explain further their conversation was interrupted by the clearing of the storm, and a cry from the shipmaster to begin boarding. The soldiers reluctantly began the business of loading the ship, which had now tied up firmly to the quayside. The Tartars seemed no less fearful than their short-legged horses, which all balked at crossing the gangplank to the bobbing deck. While they were encouraged on board, the friar spoke to the shipmaster about travelling across the Channel on his vessel. The sailor dubiously rubbed an empty eye-socket, criss-crossed with a fearsome scar, but on the production of a modest amount of coins readily agreed. Despite being a man who had been involved in many a brawl, he was still clearly glad to have a man of God on board to protect him from his other passengers. It seemed he, too, feared the devilish Tartars.

Once clear of the harbour, the strong winds struck the ship and it tossed up and down on the mountainous waves. The deck-rail was soon festooned with unhappy-looking Tartar soldiers, unused to the surface under their feet lurching so viciously. The friar decided to seek out his erstwhile companion David in order to learn more of the Tartars' mission in England. Peering down one of the dark companionways to the rear of the ship, he heard the throaty bark of two men arguing in their own tongue. He hesitated to pass the cabin from where the argument emanated in case he was accused of spying. But before he could retreat, an older man in a fur cap and a blue tunic with gold at its sleeves stamped out of the room, hotly pursued by a bare-headed younger man. The friar had seen them both on the quayside earlier, set slightly apart from the rest of the Tartars by their air of authority. He had assumed they were the party's leaders. And they looked none too friendly with each other.

The young man grabbed the other by the sleeve and spun him round, almost dislodging his cap from his head. In his other hand was a short stabbing knife which he brandished under the older man's flat nose. The friar wasn't sure whether he should intervene – the action was that of a man prepared to kill – but then the moment passed. The look of outrage and disdain on the older man's face seemed to bring the other to his senses, and slowly he lowered the knife, and let go of the other's sleeve. The older man, who the friar later learned was the leader of the Tartars, Chimbai, by name, spat at the feet of his second-in-command, Guchuluk, and disappeared into the adjoining cabin. Guchuluk suddenly seemed to realize there had been a witness to the incident, and cast a cold glance out of the corner of his eye at the dark figure of the friar that filled the doorway on to the deck. Then he, too, stepped back into his cabin. The whole set of events could not have taken more than a few moments, and the friar was left staring down the empty passage, wondering if he had dreamed it all. He returned to the open deck, deep in thought and distracted from his original aim of finding David. The sun came out, and the wind dropped, allowing the barque to settle to a more gentle undulation. But, despite the brightening of the weather, the friar had an uneasy feeling about his new companions.

After disembarking on the windy coast of England, the friar avoided the company of the two Tartar officers, who gave no outward evidence of their mutual enmity to the rest of the entourage. Instead, on the way to London, the friar fell in with a far more interesting individual. On the quayside he had looked for David, in order to beg a ride on the Tartar baggage train. But the priest was far too busy negotiating payment of the shipmaster on behalf of his masters, so the friar turned to someone else who seemed out of place in the troop of military men. He had spotted him on board the barque, looking on with amusement at the discomfiture of the seasick soldiery. His features were still Eastern in origin, but of a much more refined nature than the rest of his companions. His manner, when the friar spoke to him on the quayside, was also more civilized. He appeared unable to understand the friar's tongue, but clearly realized the import of the words, and readily agreed to the friar travelling with him on the baggage wagon.

The man tapped his chest, and spoke a melodious word or two that the friar took to be his name. Later, through the agency of David, he confirmed that he had met Yeh-Lu, a man from distant Cathay, travelling in the Tartar commander's company as administrator.

Though they discovered a mutual interest in science, there was little time for an attempt at conversation with Yeh-Lu on the trip to London. With only David to act as interpreter, and the priest not fully understanding what either man was saying, the dialogue progressed infuriatingly slowly. And David's slow recovery from the effects of the seasickness meant he showed little inclination to help them. Finally, with conversation stalled, and silence reigning, the smoky, noisome environs of London hove into view. It took for ever to whip the baggage train through the gawping crowds and over the river bridge. For the friar, used to solitude, the noise and bustle was terrifying, and the stench of so many bodies crammed together in confinement was appalling. He wondered what the Tartars thought of such an ant-hill of life. Their impassive faces betrayed nothing.

At the heart of the capital, the friar took his leave of the strange party of men, while the Tartar commander went off to negotiate his audience with Henry, King of England. He shook hands with Yeh-Lu, regretting not talking more with him. The man replied in his strange, lilting tongue:

'*Chih chen pu yen, yen che pu chih.*' He smiled at the friar's puzzled frown, and raised an eyebrow at David. The priest translated:

'It is a Chinese saying. Those who know much, talk little. Those who know little, talk much.'

Yeh-Lu clapped his hands gleefully, as though he understood David's translation. The friar nodded an acknowledgement, and took his leave of the two men. But no sooner had the

Franciscan set off on foot towards his own destination – Oxford – than he was overtaken by a flustered David on horseback. They had missed Henry by three days, and the king had left a message asking them to make their way to Oxford, where they could talk with the king's envoy and meet the king on his return from Wales. Would the friar act as their guide? He readily agreed, eager to continue his dialogue with the man from Cathay, who, despite the language difficulties, had indicated he knew of an explosive powder the nature of which also occupied the friar's curiosity.

And so he had finally completed the return journey, ten years after he had left. But, having arrived too late to enter Oxford the previous night, the friar had reluctantly to accept the hospitality of the Tartars for one more night. Now he was anxious to see the university city once again. Stepping out of the tent, he eased his aching back upright and gazed upon the city walls. They were newly built since he had left Oxford, and glowed with a golden light in the early morning sun. Though the city had once been his home for many years, he now felt a little like a stranger, standing on the outside looking in. Or, rather, looking up. The walls towered above him, and he had to squint with his tired, old eyes to discern the little figures that stood on the top. He smiled wryly to himself, wondering what the good citizens of Oxford thought of the strange encampment in the midst of which he stood. He also wondered if anything besides the walls had changed, and if there was anyone still to remember him. As if in response to the rueful thought, he imagined he heard his name being called, but from a distance.

'Roger. Is that really you?'

Emerging from the gloom of North Gate came a tall, angular figure of a man dressed in shabby, black robes. His hair was greying, and his waist tugged a little more at the belt that encircled it, but the friar had no doubt it was his young acolyte, William Falconer. Not so young now, it seemed. Friar Roger Bacon scrubbed a hand across his tonsure and the few remaining white hairs that encircled it, and wondered if he had fared so well in the intervening years. He thought probably not.

A soft light reflected off the streams and rivulets that meandered across the low-lying grasslands below the southern walls of the town. And the air itself was thick with dancing motes of dust and insects. So it was that the landscape forced a drowsiness on all those who inhabited it in these long days of summer. The excitement of the dwellers within the walls of Oxford, dulled and deafened by the contented drone of bees, had apparently not penetrated the walls of the Dominican friary that sat in the fields a little apart from the town. Here, the unhurried worship of the Creator continued at the same pace as it had done on the day before the arrival of the exotic creatures now encamped on the northern side of the town – close by, but as if a world away.

But all was not as it seemed. Friar Bernard de Genova knelt in the quiet chapel before the crucifix with head bowed, yet in his heart was a seething anger. His fellow Black Friars were about their business, many teaching in the huddle of rooms in Oxford that were the schools of the university. Bernard should have been there also, conducting repetitions on the *Sentences* of Peter Lombard. But he had a far more urgent errand to pursue, requiring a communion with the Lord.

He had been up at dawn, as was his invariable habit, and had entered the town through Little Gate as soon as it was unlocked. Once inside the town, he headed for Jewry, where the house that had been the Dominicans' first home in Oxford now served as a Domus Conversorum for those Jews converted to the Christian faith. The fact that the shabby tenement currently gave shelter to one elderly man, whose brains were addled beyond reason, did not deter Friar Bernard from taking his task seriously. He arrived every morning to take the Jew – former Jew, he reminded himself – through his Christian catechism. It was a perpetual struggle, for the old man's mind wandered, and he could not concentrate on any single thing for more than a few moments.

This morning, however, the normally vapid Bellasez was awaiting the arrival of the friar on the doorstep of the crumbling house at the top of Fish Street. His toothless mouth gaped in some semblance of a grin, and a long string of spittle hung down his sparse grey beard. He positively danced from one crippled foot to the other at the sight of Bernard. The friar was approaching sixty himself, but the pale, freckled skin of his face, contrasting severely with the black of his habit, was tight and unwrinkled. In the mornings his limbs were slower to respond, and somewhat stiff, but he still had the slender frame of his youth, and he approached his set tasks with the same vigour. He took the older man by the shoulder, feeling under his grip nothing more than skin and bone.

'Brother, what is the matter? Is something amiss?'

He steered the shambling old man back inside the house, and closed the ill-fitting door. Bellasez opened his mouth and croaked a few incoherent words. To Bernard, he resembled, despite his advanced years, a fledgling in its nest opening its gaping beak for sustenance from its parent. He sat the old man down on the only chair in the dark and stinking room, and urged calm on him. Finally Bellasez was able to marshal his thoughts sufficiently to tell Bernard what had so agitated him.

'They have returned.'

'Who have?' Bernard was puzzled, and wondered if the old man had lost his mind completely.

'I have seen them.'

The friar sighed and was about to leave Bellasez to his meanderings when the old man grabbed his arm, and said something that caused the hair on his neck to rise.

'The Ten Lost Tribes of Israel, exiled by God. They have been released, and are even now encamped outside the town.'

The friar scoffed at the old man's assertions, and sought to calm him down. It was not difficult to achieve, for soon the old man's fuddled mind drew a veil over what he had seen that morning, and he slipped back into his normal, soporific state. Bernard soon had him settled down on the smelly, straw mattress where Bellasez spent most of his days in dazed slumber, and was free to leave. Closing the door on Fish Street behind him, though, he stood pensive. The man was mad, but perhaps he was a holy fool, and his words had substance. Bernard knew what he had meant by the Ten Lost Tribes of Israel, but was not sure how he should react to the idea. It was in that moment of indecision that a youth whom Bernard recognized scurried past, excitement in his every step. William East was a promising youth to whom he had taught grammar on his first arrival in Oxford. The student was normally a solemn and serious individual, which is why Bernard, similarly inclined, had taken to him. His current state of agitation was therefore out of character.

'William East – why are you in such a hurry?'

The youth, his haste having taken him several paces past his former mentor, threw his response disrespectfully over his shoulder, in a manner that shocked the staid friar, before hurrying on his way. 'Have you not heard, Brother Bernard? There are Tartars encamped outside North Gate.'

Bernard de Genova paled. Had Bellasez spoken the truth after all? He felt a need to seek guidance.

Now, on his knees before the image of Our Lord, he pondered that very question, his thoughts as icy cold as the interior of the chapel. Though the old Jew had seen the Tartars as the lost tribes of Israel, shut away by God beyond the mountains in the East, Bernard once again was minded to listen to the words of Ezekiel, as he had done some twenty years earlier. He spoke the verses out loud:

'"This is the word of the Lord God: At that time a thought will enter your head and you will plan evil. You will say, 'I will attack a land of open villages, I will fall upon a people living quiet and undisturbed . . .' You will expect to come plundering, spoiling and stripping bare the ruins where men now live again."' The monotone of the recited words formed a whispered echo in the upper reaches of the chapel that seemed to Bernard like angels talking. And they were confirming what was echoing in the vault of his own head concerning the true identity of the Tartars now at Oxford's gate.

The slap of sandals on the cold stone slabs of the chapel floor brought him back to the mundane. Still bowed and on his knees, he tilted his head to one side. The sandalled feet at his side, the toenails of which were coarse and yellow, could only be those of Brother Adam. Though he often prayed to God to take the thought from his mind, Bernard could still not restrain a feeling of disdain for the self-centred Dominican who had been set in charge of the friary at Trill Mill after the death of Ralph de Sotell. Adam Grasse was a Breton, and, to Bernard's mind, no more than an ignorant peasant. That he had a quick mind was, in Bernard's estimation, to say merely that he was possessed of low cunning.

Adam cleared his throat at the kneeling friar's continuing lack of respect in his superior's presence.

'Brother Bernard.' The words were soft-spoken but admonitory. With a sigh, Bernard pulled himself up to his feet to face his nemesis.

'Brother Adam.'

'I have a message for you.' This immediately piqued Bernard's interest, for it would be an unusual message that Adam Grasse was prepared to deliver himself. Brother Adam, who did indeed resemble a peasant, with his vast, oval face reddened by exposure to a brighter sun than England could boast, and fat, crimson lips that caused spittle to fly as he spoke, continued, 'I have been asked to release you from your teaching duties temporarily to perform a most important task.'

Before the friar could finish, Bernard, already irritated by what had been said, interjected. 'More important than enlightening the minds of the errant youths who find their way through the course of arts study at this university, and so think themselves well versed in what matters in this world? More important than teaching them the word of God?'

Adam Grasse betrayed no annoyance on his ruddy features, merely waited until the intemperance of his brother friar had been vented, and went on. It was not for nothing that he had been selected by his fellows to be the head of the friary. His peasant frame hid a wise and calculating mind.

'You may be aware of the Tartar embassy that is encamped on the town's doorstep. Well, the king is unable to meet with them at present. Instead he has sent an envoy to speak on his behalf.'

'And how does that concern me?' Bernard marvelled at the coincidence of his conversation with God about the Tartars and Adam's reference to them so hard on its heels. But he couldn't see where he fitted into this situation.

'The envoy has specifically asked that you act as his secretary at the meetings with the ambassador.'

Bernard was still puzzled. 'Who could know me to ask specifically for my services?'

'He's here. Ask him yourself.'

Bernard looked down the aisle to where Adam's gesture pointed, and saw a ghost.

Four

. . . and you will come up, driving like a hurricane; you will cover the land like a cloud, and you and all your squadrons, a great concourse of peoples.

Ezekiel 38:9

The stone steps were worn and uneven under Falconer's feet, and he took care not to rely too heavily on the rope that spiralled up at his left hand. It was rotten and worn perilously thin in several places. He was ashamed that this was the best accommodation he could find for his friend, long separated from him. But it was cheap, and would have to suffice. He cast a glance behind him once again, as if to convince him that Roger was not an apparition. Though apparition he might be, looking at the pallor of his face and the whiteness of his hair – what was left of it – fringing his tonsure. At fifty-five, he was only a decade older than Falconer. But then Friar Roger Bacon had spent all of that decade incarcerated in a solitary cell by his order, the Franciscans, for free-thinking. Falconer hoped that his mind had not been as affected as his body. He could hear the friar's heavy breathing as he struggled up the staircase.

Hefting Bacon's small travelling satchel into his left hand, Falconer lifted the latch on the second-floor room with his right. Peering into the gloom, his heart sank. The mean, and dirty quarters smelled of rotting flesh from the skinner's yard below, and a greasy layer of dust was spread thickly on the timbers of the floor. A broken chair and scarred table were all

42

that furnished the room. Falconer looked at his friend as he leaned in the doorway, getting his breath, and an apology sprung to his lips. The friar smiled broadly.

'Ahh. This is a considerable improvement on my cell in Paris, I can tell you.' He crossed over to the narrow window, a strange three-sided structure that jutted out from the main part of the tower, and threw the shutters back. Light filtered into the room, not improving its dilapidated state. 'Look, there's a view over the river.' He peeped out of the adjacent slit like an excited child. 'And from here I can see everyone who passes on their way to the South Gate. They're quarters fit for a king, and for this I must thank you, William. I had no view at all in Paris.'

He shook the embarrassed regent master's hand, and took the satchel from him. Falconer watched as he delved in it, laying the contents out on the wobbly table. When he had recovered from the startling discovery that his long-lost friend, Bacon, had arrived with the mysterious Tartars after a ten-year absence, Falconer had been full of questions for the Franciscan. What marvels had his mind dreamed up in the intervening years? How had he fallen in with such strange travelling companions? Was he truly free of the restrictions of his order? Disappointingly, Bacon only wanted to be allowed to see Oxford again, and, having retrieved his worldly goods from the Tartar yurt, had hurried towards North Gate. Hesitating only momentarily at the sight of crowds of people, he had dived into the shambles of market stalls and shops that lined the narrow and bustling street that led to Carfax and the centre of the town. Stopping at stall after stall, he ran his fingers through the grain that the corn merchants purveyed, felt the softness of the tanners' leather, and even stopped to weigh up the relative merits of the fish laid out on the fishmongers' slabs. Just as Falconer was beginning to wonder if his great mind was turned to dust, Bacon stopped in the middle of the lane. He lifted a hand to his forehead, and frowned.

'William, can you find me some quarters? Preferably away from here.' They stood at Carfax, the junction of the roads north, south, east and west.

'Quarters? But I thought you would be returning to your brother Franciscans in the friary just outside the walls.'

Falconer saw something resembling terror flit across Bacon's troubled eyes, as though the thought of returning to his order and its rules frightened him deeply.

'No, I . . . need to be on my own.'

'But . . .' Falconer was puzzled. Here stood a man who had been in solitary confinement for ten years, and now he was saying he wanted, of his own volition, to be on his own. Bacon's look was veiled, hiding a deeper fear, and Falconer wondered how his solitary state might have affected him. He would have to go carefully, and not press his friend too quickly. He was clearly still quite delicate in mind as well as body. 'Of course – I will see what I can do.'

The search for suitable accommodation had proved difficult, especially thanks to the impecunious nature of both Bacon and his friend, the regent master. Finally, in desperation, Falconer had been referred to a skinner who plied his trade close to Grandpont. The quarters where he carried out his bloody work were at the end of the row of ramshackle houses that had sprouted up on either side of the highway running from the causeway bridge to South Gate. The building was a sort of watchtower, and the room on offer was on the topmost floor, approached by a spiral staircase. It seemed to satisfy Bacon's need for solitude while still allowing him proximity to the market, should he need it. Still, Falconer was disappointed by the poor state of the room, bearing in mind the five pence he had been required to press into the skinner's bloody hand to secure the tenure for a month.

He watched as the man who had been his mentor fussed over the few items he carried in the leather satchel that had travelled with him from Paris. After the few books that came out first, he extracted a bundle of papers, bound with cord. Falconer could see that every inch of the top parchment was covered in scribbles in Bacon's familiar hand. No doubt the rest of the documents in the fat bundle were the same. Falconer itched to ask the friar about their contents, but Bacon threw them aside as if what was written on them was insignificant. Finally, he delved into the bottom of the satchel and produced a jumble of metal wheels and lumps of lead. His face fell at the sight.

'I was afraid it would not have survived the journey.'

Falconer could make nothing of the broken pieces of metal, which included two thin wheels with regular teeth around their edges. Bacon dropped them in a heap on the table, where a long cylinder, bound with cord, rolled off the edge and landed on the dusty floor with a dull thud. The greasy motes of dust rose lazily in the morning sunshine. The friar sighed.

'I shall just have to begin again. In the mean time I have some cleaning out to do. The Augean stables have nothing on this place.' He rolled the sleeves of his woollen habit up to the elbows, and looked around for implements to carry out the cleaning. 'You might ask my landlord if he can lend me a broom and a bucket of water.'

Falconer realized he was being dismissed, and stepped towards the door, happy at least that Bacon had a task to occupy his mind. At the top of the flight of steps, he turned to say to Bacon he was truly glad to see him, but the rickety door had been firmly closed behind him

*

45

Bernard de Genova soon learned that it was no ghost he had seen in the chapel of the Dominican friary at Trill Mill. The tall, well-built man who stepped out from the shadows at the rear of the chapel was in the prime of his years. With a thick mane of blond hair framing a tanned and self-assured face, he could not have been the one who Bernard thought he was at first sight. That man would now be almost as old as Bernard. Had he lived.

Before him stood a handsome man with a long tunic of the finest linen, embroidered at the neck with gold thread. A dark blue cloak was slung casually over his broad shoulders, the hood tossed back, and a knowing smile played on his full lips. If he is not the man himself, thought Bernard, he is the very reincarnation of him. By way of explanation, the nobleman introduced himself.

'I can tell you see the family resemblance. I am Hugh Leyghton – Geoffrey was my elder brother.' He held out his hand, and Bernard grasped it. It was firm and cool.

'Then you know each other?' Adam Grasse was delighted.

The other two men laughed, but it was Hugh who spoke:

'No, we have never met. But Bernard knew my brother many years ago, and Geoffrey often spoke of him to me.'

Bernard blushed at the realization that this young man clearly viewed him as a contemporary of his older brother – some sort of long-lost uncle. For a moment he had been seduced into thinking he could revive his relationship with Geoffrey through the younger man. How foolish of him – he was just an elderly Franciscan friar to this handsome youth. An old family friend, whom it was polite to look up. He donned once again that cold, formal shell he had adopted over the last twenty-odd years in his dealings with people.

'I am pleased to meet you, my lord.' The acknowledgement of Leyghton's position and status was correct but distant, and took the knight a little by surprise. This was not the man that Geoffrey had spoken of so warmly, when Hugh had been a mere stripling. Still, the events of twenty-seven years earlier, and the intervening years, could change a man. He adopted the same formal tones.

'Brother Adam has agreed to release you to act as my secretary for the duties I must perform on behalf of the king. We must meet and negotiate with the Tartar ambassador camped on Oxford's doorstep. I am sure you and I will find the task most . . . stimulating.'

'To meet with the beast from Tartarus?' Bernard muttered under his breath. He could not be sure if this was the message from God that he had so craved in his prayers. Maybe it was, delivered, as it was, by such a comely and appropriate messenger. He saw in his mind's eye the image of Geoffrey Leyghton that had haunted him for more than twenty years. It was not the image he would have liked to have kept – of Geoffrey in full vigour – but of Geoffrey in death, hard on the defeat by the Tartars at Leignitz.

Whether Sir Hugh Leyghton, or Brother Adam, heard his bitter comment was not clear, for the knight merely continued, 'And our first duty is to be present at a banquet tomorrow night.'

The great beast stirred in the shed where it had been confined. The straw scattered on the floor of the barn was already stinking, and it had precious little room to manœuvre its vast bulk. Even if it had had space, the chains around its feet would have prevented it from stretching its stiff and aching limbs. The elephant snaked its trunk across the floor, picking fastidiously with the delicate end of its proboscis at the rotting cabbages that had been thrown in the barn for its sustenance. Though it was near mad with rage and hunger, it had learned not to push its tusks against the confining walls that restricted it so. Making a noise in such a way always resulted in its keeper beating its hide with a heavy stick with knotted cords on the end. It contented itself with rocking to and fro, rubbing its hindquarters on the rough wooden panels of its prison. Soon the spot would be a sore and open wound.

After a while the elephant heard voices outside the barn, one of them the harsh tones of its keeper. Suddenly the little door set in the bigger one opened, letting a soft evening light play on the elephant's flank, emphasizing the deep folds and wrinkles.

'Did I not tell you, master, that the beast is truly a monster?'

The swarthy keeper ushered a man and a woman into the interior of the barn, and they were both overcome by the stench of urine. The woman coughed, and held her hand over her mouth and nose. Staring into the single, mournful eye that she could discern in one side of the beast's great head, she disagreed with the animal's keeper.

'No, not a monster.' All she saw was a noble beast brought down, and was overcome with pity for the captive creature.

Still eager to please his customers, the keeper turned to the man, who was shabbily dressed in black robes, but still had the means to pay for the privilege of seeing the king's beast, gifted to him by King Louis of the Franks. 'No larger animal can be found in the world than the elephant. Persians would climb into towers on their backs and fight each other with javelins as though they were in castles. They are possessed of vast intelligence and a long memory, living for three hundred years.' Pausing but for a moment in his monologue, he cast a sly glance at the woman, and went on, 'And they copulate back-to-back.'

The woman suppressed a snigger, and the man shot her an amused but admonitory look. 'Ann!'

He turned to the keeper, and guided him towards the door. 'The agreement was that we could look at the beast alone.' Despite the man's protests, the black-robed man bundled him out of the wicket door, and closed it firmly in his face. Falconer turned a magisterial gaze on Ann Segrim, coughed tentatively, and strode over to the elephant. He peered at it closely in apparent scientific interest, nodding sagely at some inward thought of his own. Ann lifted the skirts of her gown out of the way of the stinking straw, and approached the elephant herself. Less in a mood of scientific curiosity, and more by way of sympathy, she tenderly stroked the flank of the great beast.

'William Falconer, you bring me to the most romantic spots. Peter Bullock's prison cell . . . a sweaty students' hall . . . Godstow Nunnery. And now the smelly byre of a monster.'

'You malign me,' countered Falconer. 'It was Bullock who was responsible for getting you into Godstow Nunnery. And you delighted in solving the nun's murder.'

Ann Segrim dropped a curtsey by way of ironic apology, and a stray lock of her fine golden hair fell over her pale brow. She pushed it back under the net that normally held her braids in place. 'Then I thank you for all the other memorable experiences.'

Falconer pouted. 'It was you said you regretted not seeing the elephant when it arrived. As your tutor, I simply arranged to fulfil your wish. As you heard from its keeper, we have but apocryphal stories about it. We know as little about it as . . . as . . .'

Ann supplied Falconer with an apposite simile: 'As the Tartars.'

He nodded thoughtfully.

'Then you brought me here merely to expand my education?'

That she and Falconer met as student and master had greatly improved Ann's learning, and for that she was grateful. To have her eyes opened by the great masters like Aristotle and Averroës, not to mention Galen and Bishop Grosseteste, was a relevation to her. But William seemed to think the matter between them mostly rested there. She knew there was much more to be read in the looks he gave her, but thinking was what Falconer was best at — doing came a poor second. The fact that their relationship was chaste, even when she desired it to be more, made it all the more galling that her husband assumed her desires were being fulfilled.

'What else?'

A sigh escaped her full red lips. 'Then I had better depart before we are seen together, and your reputation is besmirched.'

Falconer reddened. '*My* reputation! I thought *you* might want to avoid the gossips' tongues. And your husband's ire.' He stopped when he realized he had fallen into Ann's little trap.

In the ensuing silence, Ann continued to stroke the elephant's flank, careful not to touch the raw spot where he had been rubbing against the wooden stall. The beast seemed to quieten, and ceased its interminable rocking from one foot to the other. She wished she could soothe her husband so. Falconer spoke first:

'I have to go now.'

Hovering by the door, he awaited a response from Ann, but when there was none, he stepped over the threshold. As he left, he thought he heard her mutter, 'Poor beast,' but whether the words referred to him or the elephant, he was not certain.

Five

You shall cram yourself with fat and drink yourself drunk on blood at the sacrifice which I am preparing for you. At my table you shall eat your fill of horses and riders, of warriors and all manner of fighting men. This is the very word of the Lord God.

Ezekiel 39: 19–20

Falconer's mind was not really on the lecture he was giving that morning. And in truth neither were the thoughts of his students. Even though it was the first hour of the day, the sun was striking shafts of light through the high arched windows, drawing everyone's thoughts to what lay outside the stuffy room. The proximity of the Tartar encampment was like a magnet for the imagination of the youths sitting on the uncomfortable benches that were set facing the dais on which the regent master stood. And their teacher himself found his mind drifting away to conjecturings of creatures half-men, half-horse. Falconer tried to concentrate.

'In *de Partibus* Aristotle argues that sensation is located in the heart and not the brain. The brain, made up of colder elements, is merely the counterpoise to the heart, where heat resides, which is the essential condition of all life. In support of this, he observes, *cor primum vivens, ultimum moriens* – the heart is the first member to be formed in the unborn.'

By the third hour, the shuffling of woollen-clad bottoms, and the turning of inattentive heads almost put him off, but he pressed on.

'And in *de Generatione* he makes a most clear statement about scientific method.' He lifted a copy of Aristotle's text up to his weak eyes. 'For those of you who find Latin somewhat difficult, I will translate. "If the facts are to be sufficiently grasped, then credit must be given rather to observation than to theories. And to theories only if what they affirm agrees with the observed facts."'

He paused, for it was usually at this spot that some bright mind would attempt to deflect him on to his pet obsession – the detection of murderers using deductive logic. This time there was no interruption, and he wondered if any of the shiny faces before him had even heard his words. He was about to recommence when the door at the rear of the room was thrown open. The intrusion was so abrupt that those nearest the door cried out, assuming perhaps that the Tartars had invaded. But the intruder was someone far more familiar. His tall, skinny frame was accentuated by the ill-fitting robe that hung from it, and his pasty, freckled face was framed by a halo of spiky, ginger hair. His bony fingers wove a pattern in the air as he strove to find the right words to excuse his abrupt entry. Falconer wondered, as he always did at the sight of Nicholas de Ewelme, how such an unprepossessing man could have been appointed chancellor of the university. But such he was.

Finally, de Ewelme found his voice. 'Regent Master, I require your services as someone with a facility for languages. The king's envoy to the Tartars has insisted I accompany him to their camp this very day.'

Guchuluk watched, furious, as the old man stalked across the open meadow to the yurt where he slumbered his household gods. The young man had tried on several occasions to talk sense to Chimbai, without success. Yesterday he had been drawn into a humiliating argument with Sigatay, commander of Chimbai's personal *arban*. That it was his own fault that he found himself in such a position only served to make it all the more annoying. It was vital that he discuss the strategy for the talks with the English king with Chimbai, and the stupid old man was going out of his way to avoid him. Guchuluk wondered what he did all the time he was in the gods' yurt. Probably relived old campaigns against the Franks and the Saracens with them. The old fool was firmly anchored in the past, and that was all gone now. Gone was the time when surprise and manœuvrability on the battlefield counted for everything. Their former enemies had learned hard lessons, but they had learned. Now was the time for similar tactics, but this time at the negotiating table, in order to get the Christians on their side and against the Mamlukes. But the commander's head was in the Tanglu Mountains, and his soul fermented in *kemiz* brew.

Guchuluk sank back gloomily on to the soft skins that decorated the floor of his yurt, thinking of the impending meeting with the king's envoy that evening. It would only be a skirmish in a longer campaign, but the success or otherwise of this first encounter would set the mood for future negotiations. And whether Chimbai accepted it or not, Guchuluk knew they needed alliances now. Grimly, he resolved that, if necessary, Chimbai would have to be removed from the negotiations. He bolstered himself with remembering the final words of the Great Khan, Chinghis, spoken on his deathbed: 'My descendants will wear gold, they will eat the choicest meats, they will ride the finest horses, and they will hold in their arms the most beautiful women.' He chose not to recall the final part of Chinghis's prophecy: '. . . and they will forget to whom they owe it all.'

*

As the sun dipped redly below the battlements, the long shadow of the walls crept slowly towards the Tartar encampment. The three tents squatted like strange black mushrooms on the green fields that normally teemed with the young men who studied at the university. Their mental energies exhausted by the repetition of the learning they took in by rote, summer evenings were an opportunity to escape the confines of the city until curfew. Of course, more than a few students supplemented their meagre resources by poaching in the nearby woodland and streams, and a few heads might get cracked in the heat of the moment. But when the curfew bell called, order was generally restored.

This evening, though it was still light, and the air balmy, the fields were barren of student life. Two flaming torches, the height of a man, stood either side of one of the larger black tents, sending their sparks shooting up into the darkening sky. Besides that, there was no sign of activity around the tents other than the milling horses. Falconer felt a shiver of fear run down his back as he passed through the half-closed city gates. It was unlike him to be afraid of the unknown – indeed, he usually relished the thought of discovery. Hadn't he spent the early years of his life travelling the world in the company of merchants who plied their trade in the earth's farthest reaches? And hadn't his blood occasionally run cold at some of the situations he had found himself in? But he had never encountered a race of people with so many myths attached to them – not least the conviction that they were God's plague on mankind. He turned his gaze on Nicholas de Ewelme, who walked at his side, and was reassured that the other man looked fearful, too. He thought again of what Roger Bacon had told him when he had called to check on him that afternoon: *Men, and not monsters.*

Though it had taken some while for the Franciscan to

respond to his knocks, Falconer had been somewhat reassured by the transformation in the room, at least. After letting Falconer in, Bacon had returned to his seat at the battered table, which he had moved across nearer to the window. A simple bed, topped by a fresh straw mattress, had appeared in one corner, and the floor was now innocent of grease and grime. The watery rays of the sun lay across the surface of the table and the papers that were scattered on it. Bacon cast a glance over his shoulder at his visitor, and Falconer fancied he saw the spark of enquiry in his eyes again.

'I'm glad you came, William. I was just rereading the notes I made some years ago, when I met a most interesting character in Paris. He was a Flemish monk at the court of King Louis, and he'd just got back from Karakorum, where he had met the Great Khan of the Tartars. Oh, the sights he described, William! A palace with the walls covered in gold and silver, and pictures of dragons, beasts and birds, and an inner courtyard with trees growing in it.'

Falconer looked sceptical, because he knew how travellers, especially seamen, liked to embroider the truth until that rare commodity was stifled entirely by the embellishments that were hung on it. He had done it himself, once tempted by drink and good company.

Oblivious to his friend's gaze, Bacon went on: 'Do you know, by the way, that though we call them Tartars, they are really called Mongols. Apparently the Tartars were a minor clan defeated by the Mongols many years before they arrived in the West. But the story that they originate from the river Tar, and I suppose the tempting association with Tartarus, has served to cloud the truth. But that is not what I wanted to tell you. I recall that the monk told me of a secret formula he had learned from the foreigners at the khan's court at Karakorum. William – that was his name, too, William of Rubrouck – was told of an explosive powder by a man from Cathay. I thought you might ask Yeh-Lu about it when you see him.'

Falconer recalled the letter once sent him by Bacon, claiming knowledge of the mixture required for an explosive powder using saltpetre. Falconer had tried it out, and had nearly blown up a room full of scholars and clerics. It now seemed that Bacon had been merely guessing at the formula on the basis of second-hand knowledge. He shuddered at what might have happened.

'Yeh-Lu?'

'A most interesting fellow, with hidden depths. He hinted to me before we reached London that he knew of exploding powder, but he wouldn't reveal its secrets to me. And we did have a little problem.'

'What was that?'

'He professed not to speak any tongue I knew, and I certainly could not speak any tongue he used. We spoke through another, whose scientific knowledge was non-existent, so getting accurate information was difficult. I thought you might be able to find some common ground. After all, that's the reason why the chancellor's taking you with him, isn't it?'

Falconer wondered how a man who had only been in Oxford two days, and who had locked himself away all that time, already knew what he, Falconer, had only learned at the hour of terce. Perhaps the man was a necromancer after all. Still, he promised to do what he could for him.

As the chancellor and the regent master left the safety of North Gate and crossed the open fields towards the tents, they heard a commotion behind them. The jangle of stirrups and the thud of horses' hooves on the hard-packed mud of the lane leading through North Gate presaged the appearance of others who could only be bound in the same direction. Their importance was indicated by the fact that they planned to arrive on horseback, though their destination was but a hundred yards or so from the city walls.

Bernard de Genova was no longer used to being on horseback. He had spent many years now in Oxford, and had no need for a mount. But Sir Hugh Leyghton had insisted that they arrive at the Tartar encampment in the style befitting the king's envoy and his secretary. So it was that he found himself astride a fierce black rouncy, at the side of the noble knight who was mounted on his favourite grey charger. The streets were relatively quiet, and many stalls at this end of town were already closed, the only sign of their having been open was the litter of fish-heads and corn husk scattered across the highway. Even the taverns, normally bulging with those students who had some coin in their purses, were subdued. In the one below Bocardo, by the North Gate, a few pale, worried faces peered out as the ill-matched pair rode by. The Tartars were obviously going to be bad for trade, mused Bernard. Though he had preached endlessly against drunkenness, it had taken the arrival of the Hounds from Hell to deter the licentious.

Though it was not yet time for the curfew, the nervous watchman at the gate was worried about the city's temporary neighbours also. He had already half-closed the massive oak doors that normally barred the way to nothing worse than starving brigands and unwary wanderers after dark. As they approached, Leyghton called for the doors to be pulled back. His eyes on the Tartar encampment, the burly watchman was reluctant to obey, but eventually he began to heave on the heavy doors. Forced to wait, Sir Hugh pulled on his reins, and motioned for Bernard to do the same. Hooves clattered on the stones under the archway of the gate as the horses sensed their riders' nervousness and danced an edgy dance themselves. Leyghton leaned forward in the saddle, resting his gloved hands on the pommel.

'We need to discuss something.'

Bernard's horse stirred under his inexpert grip, and Leyghton stretched out a fist to control it for the Dominican.

'If you knew my brother, then you know how his life ended.'

Bernard felt a strange fluttering in the stone that was his heart, and for a dizzying moment he thought he might fall out of the saddle. He quickly gathered his thoughts and settled the feelings that he had suppressed for over twenty years.

'I know very well how Geoffrey died.'

'Then you must see that we now have it in our grasp to revenge him.'

The fierce look on Hugh's face contorted his natural good looks, and added years to him. Suddenly he looked even more like Geoffrey before his untimely death. Bernard took a deep breath.

'And how are we to achieve this revenge?'

'I'm not sure, but what we learn at this meeting may give us the means.' The gates were now open enough to allow the horses through, and the watchman clearly proposed to open them no further. 'Come, or we shall be late, and I am answerable to the king,' said Sir Hugh. He wheeled his horse round, releasing Bernard's reins at the same time, and cantered off across the field towards the Tartars' tents. The Dominican followed at a more sedate pace, nodding at the two black-clad scholars as he passed.

Reining in his charger in front of the group of tents, Sir Hugh sat in the saddle until the Dominican caught up with him. By the light of the two blazing torches, he could see the figure of a sentry at the entrance to one of the tents. The man, if mortal man he was, was short and stocky, his face impassive. His pock-marked features looked as though they were carved from rough stone, and the flickering light from the flames enhanced the strangeness of his flat nose and veiled eyes. Sir Hugh found himself wondering if he were real. Finally, Bernard appeared at his shoulder, yanking inexpertly on the rouncy's halter. He, too, saw the figure, and muttered a little prayer.

Suddenly the flap of the tent was lifted, and a tall, angular figure in black robes appeared. He muttered some words into the ear of the sentry, and the Tartar stepped forward to take charge of the horses. Sir Hugh slid nimbly from the back of his charger and handed the man his reins. There was a gleam of interest in the man's narrow eyes as he ran a hand over the horse's flank. Sir Hugh hoped it was in appreciation of the animal's prowess rather than of something that might make a good meal. Behind him, he heard a grunt as the Dominican got himself awkwardly off his own horse and on to the ground. Then the tall, black figure was gesturing for them to follow him between the two blazing torches and into the tent. Sir Hugh Leyghton cast a glance at the Dominican, and hoped the friar couldn't see the fear in his eyes that he could see so clearly in his companion's. He took a deep breath and followed the tall man, who held the tent flap open. By the light of the flaming torches, Leyghton recognized him as the priest who had delivered the Tartar invitation.

As the knight took a step forward, a sharp command came out of the night behind him.

'Do not step on the wooden threshold — it is a great insult, punishable by death.'

Leyghton looked back, and saw the two scholars he had

passed in the meadow, standing in the flickering light of the torches. The powerful, grey-haired one, who was obviously the man who had spoken, hurried forward.

'I have spoken to someone who travelled with these people from the coast, and he learned some of their customs. Believe me, they would strike you dead if you trod on that wooden sill.' Falconer pointed down at the innocent strip of wood, close to Leyghton's booted foot.

Sir Hugh nodded his thanks. 'Are you de Ewelme?'

'No. My name's Falconer, William F——'

The other scholar suddenly pushed himself forward, anxious to correct the error. 'I am Nicholas de Ewelme – Chancellor of the University of Oxford.' Leyghton ignored the proffered, limp hand, and regretted his demand that the chancellor of the university be present. He had hoped for another powerful man to strengthen his party, and had got a pasty-faced, ginger-haired coxcomb instead. Pity the other one – Falconer – wasn't the one in charge.

Leyghton looked hard at the two men, taking in the strength of the one and the weakness of the other, then stepped carefully over the threshold into the tent.

Peter Bullock found himself once again on the battlements, the setting sun warming his bent back. It was as if the encampment acted as a lure, drawing him to it despite himself. This evening, for example, he had intended to patrol the streets and ensure that the normally unruly students behaved themselves as the inevitability of their drunkenness progressed through the evening. Long, light summer evenings proved extremely boring for the young men who teemed in the alleys and halls of the university. On such a hot night they would normally be giving vent to their boisterousness in the meadows north of the city, but of course they were out of bounds to them at the moment. Bullock had expected the humid streets to be seething like a stew over too hot a fire. However, the streets had been unusually quiet, the mood in the innumerable taverns subdued.

He knew he should have been pleased at that state of affairs – an old soldier always prays for truces and treaties before battles, leaving the glories of death to the chain-mailed fools on horseback. But as he shambled through the narrow wynds and back alleys, where the night-stalkers were prone to lurk, he could not put off the feeling of foreboding he had had since the Tartars had arrived. The next thing he knew, he was climbing the stone steps up to the northern battlements of the city walls. And now he was peering into the circle of light cast by the burning torches in the Tartar camp. Two Western horses with saddles and halters on them were standing at the edge of the circle of light, and Bullock wondered what their riders were now witnessing in those brooding black tents.

Faint sounds of laughter drifted on the breeze, but there was no visible sign of activity. He yawned, and pulled his leather jerkin around his burly frame as the evening chill began to descend. He was too old for night vigils, and he dragged his tired limbs down the steps, into the quiet lanes of the town. All he could think of now was the comfort of his tower room in the castle keep, and the soft bed he now allowed his old bones. But his soldier's instincts had not totally deserted him, and he saw the figure that slipped quietly from one shadow to another across the end of Schools Street. He fell back into the gloom of a doorway, and observed the heavily cloaked man make his way up towards the spot on the battlements he himself had abandoned so recently. For a moment the man stepped into the yellowish light cast by a lamp that was burning late in someone's window. Bullock instantly recognized him.

'Guillaume de Beaujeu, as I live and breathe. Now what's a Templar doing in Oxford at this very moment, I wonder?'

The banquet had turned out to be no more than an excuse for an extended drinking bout by the leader of the Tartars, Chimbai. Like his compatriots, he was a short, squat man with a ruddy, moon face that glowed brighter red as the evening wore on. He wore military-style dress of a blue tunic with gold-trimmed edges, and heavy grey leggings tucked into thick, laced-up leather boots. When the English visitors arrived, he was seated on a raised couch at the back of the tent opposite the entrance. At his right hand stood a younger version of Chimbai, trying his best to look as composed and unworried. Falconer could see uncertainty in his eyes, however.

'That's Chimbai on the dais – his title's *noyan*, though I do not know what it means. And that's Guchuluk, his second-in-command, next to him, I would guess,' hissed Leyghton. 'Now you know as much as I do about this whole crew.'

Ranged around Noyan Chimbai and Guchuluk were a handful of stony-faced soldiers in similar but less ornate dress, and the man from Cathay Bacon knew as Yeh-Lu, whose long gown bore a startling pattern of colourful shapes in the form of birds and dragons. David, the Nestorian Christian priest, motioned for the Englishmen to sit on the skins that were scattered across the floor of the tent, and gestured at the pot that stood simmering on the hearth in the middle of the tent. All four men managed the unaccustomed descent to the floor with varying degrees of grace. Sir Hugh Leyghton preferred a crouch that would result in his legs aching unmercifully within a short space of time. But he suffered it in silence because he refused to fall at the feet of this barbarian, and as the evening progressed the thunder-clouds crossing his brow got darker and darker. They partook of the stew that was offered them, expressing their approval in diplomatic grunts and smiles. But Falconer noticed that Chimbai touched it not at all, preferring to suck regularly from a narrow-necked leather vessel which was never beyond his reach. As Sir Hugh got angrier and angrier, Chimbai became more and more jovial, though as yet no words were spoken. Eventually a similar vessel to that which Chimbai drank from was offered to the visitors, and Bernard de Genova took a draught from it. He grimaced, but swallowed hard, passing the vessel on to Falconer.

'Take care, it's foul,' he whispered.

The Nestorian at his elbow smiled, and explained the contents in halting Latin. 'It's a brew made from fermenting sour cow's milk with mare's milk. We call it *kemiz* – ' he threw in the guttural Tartar word for the drink. 'It's also very potent.'

Falconer drank deeply and passed the leather bottle on. It was an unusual taste that lingered on the tongue. De Ewelme, too, managed a drink without mishap, though his pasty face turned bright red. But when the flagon was passed to Sir Hugh, he drank carelessly. Immediately his face contorted, and he spat his mouthful into the fire with a roar of disgust, wiping the back of his hand across his lips.

'It's poisoned!' he roared.

There was stunned silence in the tent, which was suddenly broken by a high-pitched ululation. It came from the lips of the recumbent Tartar commander, and it was only when the other Tartars began to clap their hands in joy that Falconer realized he was laughing.

From that point on, it was inevitable that the evening would deteriorate. The Tartar commander, drunk on the heady brew of *kemiz*, issued a guttural command to the cultured-looking Oriental in outlandish robes at his feet. The man smiled modestly, and began arranging goblets and plates on the low table that stood between the commander and his guests. David moved over to Falconer's elbow and whispered in his ear.

'Yeh-Lu is from the Far East, and has learned magic from – ' he used the Latin word *baxitae*, which Falconer had never heard before. Did he mean magicians? Or priests? Falconer was soon to learn. Yeh-Lu stared intently at the goblets on the table, and the expectant silence of the other Tartars communicated itself to the small group of Englishmen. The smoky air seemed to vibrate with the intensity of concentration in the tent. Then suddenly Bernard de Genova started and cried out:

'It moved!'

Sure enough, the goblet closest to the Dominican friar began to slide across the table towards him. He fell back on his heels and made the sign of the cross, mumbling a hasty prayer. Falconer watched in fascination as another goblet moved, and another. Then suddenly two plates rose from the table and went spinning towards Sir Hugh. With a cry of horror, he dashed them to the ground with his arm. One stood spinning on its edge before it tipped and fell against its companion with a ringing sound. Once again the Tartars applauded, while, with the exception of Falconer, their guests looked on in horror. Yeh-Lu bowed his head slightly and accepted the plaudits. Only David amongst the Tartars appeared ill-at-ease, a look of pure hatred on his face for the commander who had instigated such sorcery.

Suddenly Chimbai sprang to his feet and made his unsteady way to the flap of his tent. Had the audience ended? And on such a controversial note? As the party of Englishmen got uncertainly to their feet, the commander spat out another command to Yeh-Lu. The man from Cathay smiled ingratiatingly, and stepped through the tent flap. David groaned, and spoke urgently in his native tongue to the noyan. His comments, whatever they meant, were brushed aside, and Chimbai motioned for the Englishmen to follow him outside.

The plain was now in darkness, out of which the grey bulk of the city walls loomed. The gloom was alleviated only by the guttering flames of the two torches that flanked the entrance to the tent. Between these two red columns of flame stood Yeh-Lu, an enigmatic smile upon his face. In his hands was a ball of thin rope, and, clutching one end, he threw it into the air. The rope stiffened and remained suspended, contrary to all the scientific rules that Falconer held dear. The regent master held his breath, while at his side Bernard muttered darkly of sorcery. Yeh-Lu pulled on the rope as if testing its strength, then, unexpectedly, began to climb it. There was a gasp from all those present as he disappeared out of the circle of light from the torches, and out of the sight of the onlookers. Sir Hugh Leyghton took a step forward, but was restrained by Falconer.

'I don't think we have seen everything yet,' he muttered. He had seen the malicious look in the noyan's eye. Maybe he was not as drunk as he let on.

As everyone strained to look into the darkling sky for a sight of the vanished man, something fell from the heavens. It thudded to the ground at Nicholas de Ewelme's feet, and he stared down in disbelief. It was clearly the garish sleeve of Yeh-Lu's gown – and from the end protruded the man's slender fingers. The chancellor's pale face went several shades paler, and he strove to keep down the mix of *kemiz* and stew that he had consumed inside the tent. More thuds heralded the arrival of further limbs from the heavens, then another brought the headless torso to earth. Finally a yellow, pig-tailed head fell to the ground. The consternation of Sir Hugh and his party was complete. Even Falconer was disconcerted by this development, wondering how he might solve a murder that had taken place at the top of a rope in complete darkness. As they looked on in disbelief, two Tartar soldiers scuttled around, collecting the dismembered pieces and thrusting them into a wicker basket. They then laid the closed basket at the feet of their visitors. For a moment nothing broke the stillness of the night. Then the lid flew open, and Yeh-Lu, once more in one piece, sprang from inside it. Behind Falconer the commander roared with laughter, and led the applause for his magician.

While the visitors trembled with the shock of what they had seen, Chimbai stepped in front of them, dragging the reluctant David with him. He began to orate in his harsh native tongue, only stopping when he saw David was not translating. He grabbed the scrawny priest by the collar of his robe, and shouted in his face, splashing spittle over the unfortunate man's cheeks. David paled, then bowed his head in submission. Chimbai grunted in satisfaction, and began to speak again. This time, David translated, his voice a shaky monotone below Chimbai's peroration.

'The noyan says that one day our race will rule the world from sunrise to sunset, and your king would do well to ally yourselves with him now. He says . . .' David hesitated, until Chimbai gave him a withering stare. 'He says there is no point in him or his master becoming a Christian, because Christians are so ignorant they can do nothing, while what you call idolaters can perform miracles, as you have just seen. If Chimbai were to convert, his noyans – his barons, you would say – would mock him and say, "Have you seen any miracles to Christ's credit?" And he would have to say no.'

With this, the noyan turned on his heel, and the audience was at an end.

Six

I will summon universal terror against Gog, says the Lord
God, and his men shall turn their swords against one another.
I will bring him to judgement with pestilence and bloodshed.

Ezekiel 38: 21

There were many uneasy thoughts spinning in everyone's
heads that night, and through the following day. Sir Hugh
Leyghton and Bernard de Genova had ridden off into the
night, the one to send a message to his monarch, the other to
communicate in prayer with the Almighty. Neither was happy
with what they had discovered, and both sought a means of
resolving the unusual situation. Sir Hugh had intimated to the
friar that they should meet the following morning in order to
plan what their common strategy should be. In the light of
their meeting with a race of men they both had reason to hate,
this promised to be a difficult encounter.

Nicholas de Ewelme had accompanied Regent Master
Falconer back across the plain below the walls, and entered
through Smith Gate, as prearranged with Peter Bullock, the
constable. Neither man spoke at first, but Falconer could tell
that the chancellor was deeply disturbed. As a cleric, de
Ewelme was outraged at Chimbai's rejection of Christianity;
as the administrator of a great university, he was fearful of the
devastation the Tartars could mete out – had, indeed, already
rendered to accumulated knowledge throughout the rest of
Christendom. But what could he do to prevent their incursion
into England, and, more precisely, into Oxford? He was no

warrior. But on the other hand he was adept at manipulating people and circumstances – how else had he won the coveted post of *cancellarius Oxonie*, university chancellor, against the opposition of others more erudite and worthy? Perhaps a certain amount of manipulation could have some severe consequences for the heathen Tartars in this circumstance. He was incautious enough to voice his opinions to Falconer.

'Something will have to be done about this. We cannot allow the king to be taken in by these . . . these monsters.'

'Monsters, Chancellor? Some were calling that poor beast of an elephant a monster only a few days ago. And look at it now – languishing in its own ordure and a harm to no one.'

De Ewelme was shocked by Falconer's lack of understanding of the situation. He had been warned about this regent master by one of his predecessors, Thomas de Cantilupe, who had told him the man was headstrong and rebellious. He had been prepared to make up his own mind about him, rather than taking someone else's opinion – especially someone like de Cantilupe, to whom the epithets headstrong and rebellious could be applied in equal measure. But it seemed de Cantilupe was right, and Falconer was not to be trusted. Now that opinion was well and truly confirmed, he abruptly closed off the regent master from his confidences. He would simply have to make the Tartar embassy untenable on his own, and he thought he knew a way of so doing. As Bullock locked the small wicket door set in the massive Smith Gate behind the two university men, Nicholas de Ewelme mumbled his good-nights and scuttled away into the darkness.

Inside the Tartar camp itself, there were those who were equally disconcerted by Chimbai's actions. Yeh-Lu was tired of acting as Chimbai's tame monkey, performing his silly tricks whenever called upon to do so, and the Nestorian priest, David, was increasingly perturbed by the noyan's dismissal of

68

Christianity. Many of the ruling family in Karakorum were converting to Christianity, and though David knew some of it was for diplomatic reasons, he had cause for optimism. Yeh-Lu, for his part, had a mind to create more serious marvels than simple sleight-of-hand could provide. However, the saying *chi pu tse shih* came into his drowsy head – beggars can't be choosers. Both men felt impotent to act in the claustrophobic confines of the encampment, and both laid sleepless heads on the furs of their beds.

But chief among the worriers was Guchuluk, who was convinced that his superior had ruined any chance of gaining the support of the English king. He had seen the black and angry look on the face of the king's ambassador as he had ridden off into the night. He was sure Leyghton was not going to respond to a show of strength and unconcern such as Chimbai had displayed. And he was equally sure that such strength was not theirs to wield any longer. He paced the few yards between his sleeping furs and the edge of the fire that glowed redly in the centre of his yurt. His mind was in turmoil, and he ignored the uneasy stares of his men-at-arms, who could not themselves retire until he had settled for the night. Staring into the embers of the fire, he pondered his position. The more vigorous elements of the Il-Khan's court in Persia had elected him to represent them to the kings of England and France, but, as a last rearguard action of the old order, he had been saddled with the monster Chimbai as his superior. He was now certain that it was time to rid himself of the monster.

'So, tell me what they are like, William. Did they offer you human flesh to eat?' Bullock's lined face was aglow with eagerness to hear the details of Falconer's encounter with the Tartars. If possible, the more gruesome the better. He had followed the regent master back to Aristotle's Hall on the pretext of protecting him from night-stalkers, though both men knew full well that Falconer was capable of taking care of himself. He had ascended to Falconer's solar at the scholar's heels, and now he refused to leave until his friend had given him some juicy titbit of information. Falconer smiled to himself.

'The meat in the stew was rather tough, so it could have been old soldier.'

Bullock snorted with disdain, but would not abandon his quest for titillation. 'Didn't they even serve mare's blood to drink?'

Falconer was tired, and a little tetchy. 'No, Peter. But they did cut a man to pieces, and restore him to life again. Nothing unusual, really. So I wish you goodnight.' With this he slammed the solar door on the bewildered constable, who was so surprised he forgot to tell Falconer about seeing the Templar de Beaujeu in the town. Behind the door, Falconer dropped down on to his bed, falling asleep almost immediately. He dreamed of dismembered bodies that rose and walked again, unaware that on that night the inexorable process that would lead to one man's death had already begun.

The next few days in Oxford saw life almost return to normal on the surface. Idle students still went to gawp at the Tartars from the city walls, but the honest and hard-working citizens had little time for such indulgence. The markets in Oxford's cluttered streets gradually regained their normal bustle. Hearty curses rang down the lanes as incautious visitors were jostled in the throng and stepped into the stinking sewer channel that ran down the middle of the streets. It was only later that many would find they had lost their purse as well as their dignity. The outbreak of cut-purse activity kept the constable, Peter Bullock, too busy to think any more about the proximity of the Tartars and the threat they might hold for Oxford's safety. It took him a full day of patient observation before he spotted the culprit at work. Or rather, culprits, because there were two who worked together at relieving honest citizens of their hard-earned coins. One, a burly youth, would jostle a likely candidate's elbow. Then, under the pretext of apologizing and setting the mark back on his feet, he would lift his purse from his sleeve or pocket and slip it behind him, where his accomplice was passing. The accomplice, a thin boy — no more than a child, really — wandered on his way, innocently whistling, while the first cutpurse engaged his mark in conversation. If the mark suspected anything of the burly youth, and had him searched, there would be nothing to show for it but embarrassment. But the old campaigner, Bullock, had seen it all before. After checking he was right by watching the clever little juggling act twice, and admiring the skill involved, he grabbed both perpetrators by their greasy jerkins at the moment of exchange on the third attempted theft. A surprised and very relieved merchant recovered his purse from the ground where it had fallen, and Bullock hurried the youths off to his gloomy cell under the gaze of a derisive crowd.

Meanwhile, the target of people's interest but a few days earlier was giving any onlookers precious little to stare at. The encampment was unusually quiet during the day, except for occasional forays into the woodland by a single soldier on horseback, who would soon return with something furry laid across his horse. The squat little men on their squat horses were obviously adept at replenishing their food stocks from the local wildlife. And if anyone had reason to complain about this depredation of good food resources, the Tartar horsemen's inscrutable stares soon deterred them.

Falconer continued his daily routine of cramming education

into the skulls of farmers' sons and barons' nephews. His only distraction now was that he was a little worried about Roger Bacon. The friar had virtually locked himself away in the turret over the skinner's that he had quickly adopted as his home and workshop. In response to Falconer's calls, he had only once briefly appeared at the door, a pale face thrust in the narrow gap that was all he allowed as an opening.

'William! I'm sorry, but I'm terribly busy at the moment. Would you mind if I didn't ask you in?'

Falconer had acquiesced, and was abruptly left facing a firmly closed door. He was about to leave when, behind it, he thought he heard the voice of another man. He put his ear to the cracked and roughened surface of the door, but all he could hear was a strange and regular clicking noise. So he was provided with no greater clue as to what was afoot behind it. More than a little upset that someone he considered his closest friend and mentor should abandon him only days after returning from a ten-year absence, he nevertheless still kept an eye on Roger. Each evening he made a point of walking along Grandpont as part of his regular perambulation. And each evening he saw flickering candlelight emanating from the narrow slits that served as windows at the top of the look-out tower occupied by Roger. During the day, he saw neither hide nor hair of the friar. Then one evening, towards the end of the week that marked the arrival of the Tartars, he saw something very unusual.

He had walked the length of the High Street, deep in thought, and found himself close under St George's Tower on the perimeter of the castle keep. The castle stood at the western end of the city, and was the home of his friend the constable. It also temporarily housed the king's great beast – the elephant – which was still on public show. The evening was still light, with a cooling breeze blowing off the marshes south of the city. Falconer decided, on a whim, to look at the elephant again. As he approached the barn where he had last seen it with Ann Segrim, he heard a great commotion. Spilling out of the small gateway set in the barn door came a group of students, all the worse for drink. They raced across the yard, whooping and yelling, only pulling up short when they recognized the stern features of the regent master. They walked past him with the wooden dignity of the drunk, wishing him a good night, only spoiling their performance when they had passed him by breaking out in a fit of giggling. A wry smile crossed Falconer's lips as he recalled his own youth, which had been far wilder than these youngsters', did they but know it.

As he stepped over the threshold into the barn, the gloomy interior robbed him of vision for a moment. The keeper of the elephant, more usually at the entrance and keen to impress each visitor to his monster, seemed not to be in evidence. Then Falconer's eyes began to adjust to the darkness, and the smell inside the barn assailed his nostrils. The beast was not on its feet but huddled in a great mound in the dirty straw that surrounded it. It somehow seemed shrunken from its previous impressive size, its wrinkled skin slack on the massive bones that lay under its surface. Falconer heard a snuffling sound, and at first assumed it was the beast who was making it. Then he saw the elephant's keeper. He was draped across the elephant's head, clutching at both great ears, and he was weeping. Falconer waded through the stinking straw, and the man wailed at his approach.

'Leave him alone. You – you monsters.'

Falconer assured him the students had gone, and clutched the man's arm, gently drawing him away from the elephant. There was a long gash on the beast's head just below its huge, mournful eye. Falconer was entranced for a moment by how the long lashes around its eye made it look vulnerable and ladylike. The gash was oozing blood.

'What happened here?'

The keeper shrugged. 'Those youths decided they wanted to know if the beast was unnatural or not. Whether it was a monster. So one of them took out his knife and . . .' He gestured at the vicious wound, then attempted to wipe his tears away. 'Well, now they know he bleeds like any other of God's creatures.'

The straw at the beast's feet rustled as it shook its great frame, and Falconer watched in wonder as a great shudder ran through it. How soon had the marvel that was this beast become just an idle curiosity, exactly like the Tartars. It was said the elephant lived three hundred years, and conceived by eating the mandragora root in Paradise. Falconer did not believe any of this, but nor did he know anything truthful about this wonderful beast's life. What value was scientific observation now, in this stinking barn, so far from the creature's natural home? As if remembering its place of birth, the beast gave forth a sigh as massive as its frame, and settled further into the straw that was its bed. Falconer left the distraught keeper to comfort his charge, at a loss as to what to do to help.

Turning down Fish Street, Falconer hurried towards South Gate, anxious to keep up his surveillance of the troubled Roger Bacon before the curfew closed the gates against him. The distraction with the elephant had delayed him, and so he was late reaching the stretch of Grandpont bridge that ran over the river and marshy land outside the gate. If he had arrived at his normal time, he might not have seen whom he did leaving the friar's tower. The figure was shadowy, slipping from the gloomy doorway at the bottom of the tower to the back of the row of hovels that lined the road, but the coat made the man's identity unmistakable. As Yeh-Lu's dragon-clad form skirted the city walls on its way back to the Tartar camp north of the city, Falconer wondered what his business had been with Roger Bacon. He had a mind to question the friar immediately, but he could see from where he stood that there was no light in the tower. Reluctantly, he saved his curiosity for the morrow and returned to Aristotle's Hall and a fitful sleep.

Guillaume de Beaujeu, Commander of the Poor Knights of Christ and the Temple of Solomon, more usually known as the Templars, was, by contrast, wide awake. But then he was a creature of the night, his special skills learned in Outremer – the Holy Land that his order was pledged to defend – and used at the Grand Master's behest. It did not always please him that he was so much used as a mindless weapon; obedience was one of the rules he followed with difficulty. Still, he was single-minded, and determined to be a fitting Grand Master himself one day, though the very idea was no doubt a contravention of the order's rules on pride and arrogance.

Oxford was a city he knew well, which made his task easier to some extent, as he could make use of his knowledge of the layout of lanes. On the other hand, the very fact that he was known here could work against him in the peculiar circumstances in which he found himself. His presence was not to be made known to anyone. And that was why he was limiting himself to nocturnal activity, and languishing by day in the poor hovel of an inn he had found in Torold's Lane. Used to the spartan but clean comforts of the Golden Ball Inn, his present accommodation was a filthy room in the stinking house that appeared not to even merit a name. The sign outside had long ago given in to the depredations of the weather, and was nothing more than a bare, pale wooden board with a few indecipherable strokes marking its surface. He hoped its very anonymity had brushed off on himself – he needed to be invisible for the next few days.

He crept silently out of the front door of the inn, taking care not to open it wide, for it creaked if it was opened more than half-way. Looking to left and right, he was reassured there was no one in the lane, and he pulled the door closed behind him. Though the hour was late, the air was clammy, making the night almost as hot and sticky as the day, and it brushed against his face like a damp curtain. He slunk along under the overhang of the upper floors of the houses in the lane – each leaning towards its neighbour across the street like drunken companions. His mind tossed around the conversation he had had with the Grand Master only a week or so before.

The meeting had taken place in the austere surroundings of the Temple in Paris, its echoing and chilling interior a reflection of the soul of the Grand Master himself. Guillaume had been summoned to his presence with an indication that his skills were required once again. With leaden feet, he trudged to the chapel where he had been told the old man was praying, and he found him on his knees before the altar. The old man's white-haired, tonsured head was bowed, and de Beaujeu stood patiently at the back of the chapel. Remaining still for hours on end was one of his particular skills, so it was no great problem to put off the inevitable for a little while longer. Eventually the Grand Master rose, crossed himself, and turned to address his acolyte. At the sight of his face, de Beaujeu was astonished – the master's eyes, normally so cold and merciless, were ablaze with an unaccustomed exultation. He positively hurried across the bare stone space between himself and de Beaujeu, barely able to contain what it was that had lighted up his soul.

'Guillaume, I have the Lord's work for you.'

The words sent a chill down de Beaujeu's spine – such an injunction usually presaged the demise of some poor soul at his hands. As if to confirm his worst fears, the master put his hand on de Beaujeu's arm, and he could tell it was trembling.

'It concerns Those from the East.' The Grand Master had never allowed the word 'Tartar' to pass his lips since the Order of which he was now the head had encountered the scourge that was the Tartar army near Leignitz over twenty years earlier. Ponce d'Aubon, the Grand Master who had preceded the present incumbent, had reported on the slaughter of the flower of northern Europe's chivalry then, including the horrific fact that, after the battle, 'Those from the East' had cut an ear from each body as a counting device. They had filled nine sacks to return to their khan.

The Grand Master paused, as if to give greater significance to what he was about to say, and looked furtively around. The cloister in which they walked enclosed a garden full of sweet herbs that filled the summer air with enticing scents. Thyme, rosemary and anise thrived under the tender fingers of the monastic gardeners. But the light aromas were in complete contrast to de Beaujeu's heavy heart, and the aura of sweetness jarred with the Grand Master also. What secrets he had to tell were better conveyed in the gloom of a private chamber, and he led de Beaujeu back to his austere quarters, dismissing the personal clerk and valet which was all the Templar order specifically allowed him as master.

As de Beaujeu made his silent way down the lanes that led to Smith Gate on the north side of Oxford, he recalled his own astonishment at what the Grand Master revealed to him in that dark and gloomy chamber far away from the light and warmth of the herb-scented Parisian garden. The white-haired old man went straight to a locked, iron-bound chest that stood on the heavy table in the centre of the room. He produced a key from his purse, inserted it, and turned it in the lock. As master, he was one of the few Templars who were allowed the luxury of being able to lock possessions away. Lifting the heavy lid, he delved in the chest and produced two documents. One was fresh and new, with a recently broken seal on it. The other was ancient, the parchment creased so much that the document was almost separated into several pieces along the folds. Careless of the damage he might be doing to the second document, the Grand Master waved both in the air triumphantly.

'At last we have the means to regain the Holy Lands, and resolve the matter of the Tartars at a stroke.'

De Beaujeu was so surprised to hear the word 'Tartar' pass his master's lips that he could hardly take in what the old man then told him. Now, however, he stood at Smith Gate on the threshold of carrying out this monumental task, which would be of such great importance to the Templar order.

For the past few evenings he had strolled past the gate and observed the gatekeepers who sat at their post into the night. If the occasion allowed, he entered into conversation with them. All of them were elderly men of a variety of temperaments, carrying out their task with different capacities. One was still alert, despite his age, another grumpy and regretful that the only means he had of earning his living was to give up the solace of a warm bed at night. Neither gave him the opportunity he needed.

Tonight was different. The old man who sat at the gate resembled a skeleton, his skin drawn tight over his old bones. An enormous wen grew from the top of his head, protruding through the sparse thatch of his hair. More importantly, his head nodded down into his chest, pointing the mottled wen at any passers-by. A leather bottle lay empty at his feet – a clear indication of the cause of the gatekeeper's stupor. De Beaujeu approached cautiously, but a stertorous snore confirmed that the old man would not be easily disturbed. Gently, he slid his fingers round the key-ring that hung at the gatekeeper's waist, and he lifted the key to Smith Gate off his belt. The old man's head jerked, and de Beaujeu froze, but gradually the head returned to its former position, the wen bobbing up and down rhythmically with the man's breathing. Swiftly, de Beaujeu was through the gate, leaving the key in the lock for his return journey. His crossing of the meadow towards the Tartar encampment would have gone completely unnoticed, if Peter Bullock had not found it difficult to sleep, and had not been stalking the top of the city walls when he should have been abed.

Seven

Say, These are the words of the Lord God: I am against you,
Gog, prince of Rosh, Meshech and Tubal . . .

Ezekiel 38:3

The bow was strung, and the arrow set in place, its sharpened tip glowing dully in the light of the tallow lamp. The bow was a mighty weapon, stronger than the English longbow, and capable of a range of over three hundred yards. The layers of horn, wood and sinew that made up the bow were stretched so that the semi-circle of the unstrung bow, when strung, was pulled back on itself, with the ends curved away still from the archer. When released, the horn would snap back to its original shape, shooting the arrow with far more power than an ordinary wooden bow. The arrow was a short-range arrow with a tip that had been hardened by plunging it into salt water when red-hot. It wouldn't need to travel far. The string of the bow was pulled back by a stone thumb-ring that all the Tartar soldiers used. It was a difficult technique, but provided far more accuracy. In this case, the bow was already aimed squarely at the target, and it only remained for the right time to come.

That was provided by the early-morning arrival of Noyan Chimbai at his private tent, housing the supreme god Tengri. Safe in isolation, and guarded by three of his retainers, who surrounded the tent and made it impossible for anyone to disturb the noyan at his devotions, Chimbai performed his daily ritual of offering food and water to the god and his concubines, then stood in obeisance before their felt images. His hearing had been poor for a number of years, but he had hidden it, and supposed no one knew of this weakness. So he did not hear the strange sound inside the tent that would otherwise have alerted him to a presence other than this own. At the preordained moment, the Tartar thumb-ring slipped the string. The string straightened abruptly under the pressure of the powerful bow, and sent the projectile on its way. It cut through the air with a faint whistling sound, then thudded into its target. The armour-piercing arrow ripped through Chimbai's outer quilted jacket as though it did not exist. Once through that layer, it encountered his inner cuirass of boiled and lacquered leather strips that he habitually wore. In battle this layer might deflect a sword thrust or swung at Chimbai, but it was no match for the direct path of the hardened arrowhead. With its progress hardly slowed, the arrow continued on its course. The final layer of clothing on the noyan's body was a silk shirt. This was no affectation of luxury. If an arrow had been slowed sufficiently by the layers of armour as it spun onwards, the silk would wrap itself around the head and be pulled into the wound. Many a soldier's life had been saved by gently pulling the silk and arrow-head out of the wound. This arrow was travelling too swiftly for the silk to have any such effect. The cloth was no more effective than a layer of paper, and the arrow drove on into the skin beneath it. Finally it plunged into his chest, through his still pumping heart and on out of the layer of flesh and skin on his back, only being stopped there by the selfsame layers of clothing that had proved ineffective over Chimbai's chest. The whole process took but a few moments, and came as a nasty and quite fatal surprise to him.

Eight

His struggle with the great horned monster was a one-sided affair. The muscles of his arms popped and cracked with the exertion as he strove to encompass the creature's muzzle. He knew that, if he let go, the sharp, yellowed teeth that filled its mouth would tear him apart in an instant. The breath that it exhaled from its flared nostrils was hot and foetid on his face, and he grimaced in horror. As the two of them swayed back and forth, locked in mortal combat, the monster's glittering, curved horn which protruded from the centre of its scaly face threatened to gouge out Falconer's eyes. He could feel his strength draining from him, and the monster's feet were drumming in triumph on the dusty earth. His mind fled his body, and he snapped awake in the familiar surroundings of his own solar.

He sat up, hot and sweaty, and untangled the coarse blanket that was wrapped around his limbs. Then he realized that the drumming sound was real, and it was coming from downstairs. Someone was knocking at the street door of Aristotle's Hall. Pulling on the black robe he had carelessly thrown across his work-table the previous night, he stumbled out of the room, and down the creaking stairs.

Attempting to pick off a mass of red kite feathers that had somehow stuck to his robe, he threw the door open on his early-morning visitor. The figure lurking nervously in the doorway had a large brown cloak pulled around him, with the fur-lined hood well over his face. Falconer thought it odd to be so attired in the warmth of what promised to be another sticky summer's day. He peered short-sightedly into the shadow cast by the hood and was surprised to recognize the oriental features of Yeh-Lu. He was even more surprised when the man from distant Cathay spoke to him.

'Please let me in.'

It was a moment before Falconer realized he had spoken in English. He stepped back and ushered the man of many surprises into the communal hall of Aristotle's, which Falconer shared with the students in his charge. One curious youth, Richard Youlden, poked his sleepy face over the banister rail that ran across the upper end of the hall. Rubbing his eyes, but not really taking in who the early-morning visitor was, he gladly disappeared back to his bed on being told by the regent master that he had dealt with the intruder.

Falconer turned back to Yeh-Lu, surprised to see that the man, so cautious out in the street, had pulled his hood from his face in the presence of Richard Youlden. Even so, the lad, a farm boy from the north, could not have seen him, or he would have roused the whole hall by now. It had been a very indiscreet act by a very circumspect individual. But then, Yeh-Lu did look anxious, and perhaps he had acted thoughtlessly because of it. Falconer pointed to a chair, and mimed that Yeh-Lu should sit, before remembering that his visitor had spoken to him in English.

'Please sit – and tell me how you know our tongue.'

Yeh-Lu smiled wearily as he slumped into the high-backed chair that stood by the cold and dusty hearth. 'This is not the first time I have encountered Englishmen. When I first began to serve at the Il-Khan's court more than twenty years ago, I met a man who had been exiled from his native land of England. It was said he was a member of the Order of the Poor Knights of the Temple.' Yeh-Lu looked quizzically at Falconer, as if to confirm such an organization did exist. Falconer nodded. So Yeh-Lu had encountered a Templar knight, and a renegade one at that. And if he had served at the Tartar court in Persia for twenty years, he was older than he looked. He gestured for the man to continue.

'The man was thoroughly unpleasant, parading the superiority of his own faith before everyone. But he would never explain why his religious brothers had ejected him from their company. Hulegu – the Lord khan at the time – used him for errands that required use of the man's own tongue, and, though they were only menial tasks, the man inflated them into major diplomatic missions. Hulegu soon tired of him and sent him on a bogus mission to the khan of the North. I understand the man was later captured in Austria, and executed by one of your warrior lords. Rightly so, of course, for you can never trust a turncoat. But while he was at Hulegu's court, I persuaded him to teach me his language. He was greedy for gold, so he was not difficult to persuade.'

Falconer still stood over the foreigner, who, slumped in the chair, looked smaller than he had done when performing his magic tricks before Sir Hugh Leyghton. He may have learned his English twenty years before, but it was perfect, though spoken with a strange lilting accent. Falconer wondered what the sallow-faced man wanted of him, that had driven him to brave discovery at the gates of Oxford. No one would have been keen to admit a Tartar to the town, and he might even have been attacked if uncovered.

'Why are you here?'

Yeh-Lu's face betrayed deep concern. 'It's your friend, Roger Bacon.'

'What of him?' Falconer asked, thinking that the man spoke of Bacon like a colleague.

'I fear there is something wrong. You see, I was intrigued by the breadth of his knowledge when we talked on the journey to Oxford. And since then I have visited him more than once in his tower. It is very convenient that it is outside the city walls.'

Falconer realized his sighting of Yeh-Lu in the vicinity of Bacon's tower the previous night had clearly not been the only time the man had been there. He wondered if it had been Yeh-Lu who had been in Bacon's room the time he had been snubbed by his friend. He also wondered what knowledge they had shared and what they might have been up to. But Yeh-Lu obviously wasn't going to enlighten him on that matter. However, he did say he had gone to Bacon's eyrie early this very morning, and had got no response to his knocks on the door.

'I am worried that something may be amiss. He is, after all, not in the best of health.'

Yeh-Lu was beginning to worry Falconer now. He didn't want to be reunited with his old friend only to have him snatched away by illness, even if Bacon had been behaving oddly with him of late. Both men hastened towards the door, Yeh-Lu pulling the fur-trimmed hood of his cape up over his shiny black hair. They hastened in silence through the narrow back streets towards South Gate. The area was populated largely by students, but as the morning sun had hardly begun its climb into the pale blue sky, few people had yet stirred. It was a different matter as they turned out of St Frideswide's Lane into Fish Street. There the traders were opening up their shop fronts, and the buzz of a normal day had already begun.

Here and there the black-clad figures of Jews could be seen hurrying towards the synagogue, which was squeezed in among the narrow houses opposite St Aldate's Church that made up part of Oxford's Jewry.

Yeh-Lu drew his cloak closer around him, which in truth drew him almost as many curious stares on this warm morning as if he had gone undisguised. Near the gateway, a beggar pulled at his cloak, entreating alms, and the hood slipped back to reveal his oriental face. But luck was with Yeh-Lu. The blind beggar stared with eyes as white as a seethed egg, and the moment of danger was gone. Falconer thrust a coin into the poor man's outstretched hand, and Yeh-Lu yanked the hood back over his features.

They negotiated the ramshackle hovels outside South Gate without another mishap, and Falconer's long legs took him swiftly up the spiral staircase to Bacon's tower room. He hammered on the door, almost expecting to have to break it down, and was therefore taken aback when, moments later, the door was opened. The friar's wrinkled face appeared, his halo of sparse hair sticking out as though he had just risen.

'William! What's so amiss that you have to hammer on my door so early? The sun is barely up over the trees. And, as you look out of breath, I assume you have run here in order to apprise me of whatever it is that could not wait.'

The friar stood squarely in the crack of the door as before, not allowing his visitors to see the interior of his cell. Though, if what Yeh-Lu had told Falconer was true, the man from Cathay had on more than one occasion gained admittance to Bacon's inner sanctum himself. Bacon seemed nervous and anxious to return to whatever task it was that awaited him behind the firmly held door. Falconer had the fleeting image of him standing thus to bottle up a demon he had invoked into his presence. With some embarrassment, he realized he had just slipped into making the same suppositions that the folk of Oxford and Bacon's own order had made about his scientific endeavours ten years before. Bacon had been accused of being a necromancer, and a creator of unnatural life in mockery of the Lord.

'Forgive us, dear friend.' It was Yeh-Lu, standing on the lower step below Falconer, who apologized for their peremptory appearance. 'I knocked earlier and got no reply. I was worried about you, and remembered you telling me of your friend Falconer, and where he lived. I took a chance, and went to find him. It seems I have woken two people unnecessarily. Once again I apologize.'

Sigatay, commander of Chimbai's personal *arban*, was a worried man. He was under strict instructions from the noyan that he should not be disturbed by anyone. Sigatay took 'anyone' to include himself, and he had never dared venture into Chimbai's sacred yurt. But the general usually spent no more time in there than it took for the sun to rise the height of a man. Today, he had been in there much longer, and the sun was now high in the sky. Sigatay could see a few curious faces staring down at the Tartar encampment from the supposed security of the city walls. He had a passing thought of other apparently impregnable walls that had fallen before him and his men in the past, and he gave out a high-pitched hiss of satisfaction. He wished he were even now embroiled in some life-or-death struggle with a visible enemy. Decision-making in such circumstances was simple. Now he had to decide between the wrath of his master at being interrupted, or the unimaginable error of ignoring his master's need for assistance. He glanced nervously at the two other men he commanded. Both stood impassively in stony silence, though Sigatay knew that inside their leather-clad breasts they were relieved that the impossible decision was not theirs to make.

Sigatay frowned in unaccustomed concentration. Then, deciding that no one could have got near the noyan to do him any harm, he grunted in satisfaction and remained at his post. He was unaware, of course, that Chimbai's heart had long ago been stilled by an arrow. And that his life's blood was already congealing into the intricate designs of the fine and elaborate rugs that decorated the yurt's floor, adding another, more random swirl of colour to their patterns.

The Dominican friary rose on an island set in the marshy land just beyond the hovels huddled on the southern edge of Oxford. Outside the friary walls, the low-lying ground was rumoured to be inhabited by ghosts and demons (though those of a scientific bent would maintain the apparitions were merely the effulgence of marsh gases). Inside the friary, set between Trill Mill Stream and the river, everything was well ordered, and devoted to the worship of the Lord. Though the Black Friars abhorred the remote contemplation of the older monastic orders, they still observed the routines of worship that separated the day into matins, terce, sext, nones and vespers. It caused some alarm to his fellows, therefore, that Brother Bernard de Genova was conspicuously absent from the chapel throughout the morning.

About the middle of the day, just before sext, Adam Grasse was informed of this absence. He agreed that the grave error on Bernard's part required investigation – the man, after all, might be ill. Availing himself of his seniority, but not without trepidation, he agreed to enter Bernard's cell. He knew that if there proved to be no good reason for him having done so, he would have made an enemy for life. Bernard de Genova valued

88

his privacy — in so far as a friar of the Dominican order could. None the less, the circumstances were so unusual that Grasse felt justified in invading what little privacy any Dominican was allowed. Filled with a sense of foreboding, he waddled along the cloister to where Bernard's cell was located, breathing heavily through his open mouth at the unaccustomed exertion. Behind him, like a gaggle of goslings following their overweight mother, scurried those Black Friars who had got wind of the possible scandal. Brother Bernard was a stand-offish man, who had found few friends and allies in his ten years at the friary, and rumours of past indiscretions had followed him from his last post in the north. If he was now to be embarrassed, or even disgraced, there were several of his so-called brethren who wanted to be present. Their hopes were to be dashed.

Adam Grasse tentatively called Bernard's name at the closed door of the cell, knocking softly with his fat fingers. When there was no reply, he lifted the latch and stepped inside, closing the door firmly against the prying eyes of his fellow Black Friars. The room had only one unglazed slit of an opening, high on the wall to the left of the door, and, facing north, it gave precious little light. Bernard had personally selected the cold and uncomfortable room, even though his seniority in the order spared him the dormitory and might have allowed him less spartan surroundings. Whatever reason it was that had caused him to choose this room was known only to Bernard himself and Grasse's predecessor, Ralph de Sotell. Grasse was unaware of whether it was some sort of self-inflicted punishment, and if it was, what perceived sin had occasioned it. Though Grasse was confessor to his brethren, Bernard had not availed himself of this service since the fat Breton's appointment. Bernard appeared only to voice his fears and worries directly to God.

As Grasse's eyes adjusted to the gloom of the cell, he

became more aware of his surroundings. And at first sight there was nothing to distinguish it from any other friar's cell. A large crucifix hung on the lime-washed walls directly over the head of the narrow bed, with its thin mattress. The only other furniture was a simple lectern that stood in one corner. It was set below the window slit, so that whoever used it might read by the thin beam of light that filtered into the cell, thus economizing on candles. Adam Grasse was disappointed – there was nothing in the room to suggest anything unusual had happened to Bernard de Genova. He scanned the room and its furniture again, though certain that he could not have missed anything in such a bare cell. When his eyes lit upon the bed, he suddenly realized he had. Everything else in the cell spoke of a fastidiously neat man, living an ordered life. And at first sight the bed confirmed that. But on closer examination the threadbare blanket that lay atop the mattress was crumpled, as if pulled hurriedly into place. Holding his breath, Grasse leaned over the bed, and lifted the blanket. Underneath, the surface of the mattress was freshly stained with a copious amount of blood.

It was now nearly the middle of the day, and Yeh-Lu still clung to the companionship of William Falconer. It seemed that, having made his acquaintance, the Oriental was somehow reluctant to give it up. He had heard of the ailing elephant and had persuaded the regent master to smuggle him back in through the South Gate and show him where the beast was stabled. At least the daytime bustle of Oxford made their return through the gate less dangerous than their early-morning passage had been. Used to the eccentricities of travellers in this crossroads of a town, no one questioned the stranger who was wrapped in cloak and hood as though the warm and sticky day were in fact a crisp winter's morning. As they passed the market stalls in Fish Street, the traders called the attention of the two men to the quality of their wares, and were ignored. But they were used to that, and rapidly switched their sales pitch to the next passer-by. When they entered the castle grounds, Falconer glanced nervously up at St George's Tower. If Peter Bullock were in residence, he would have apoplexy at Falconer's insinuation of a Tartar into the central defence of the town. He took Yeh-Lu's arm, and hurriedly propelled him to the barn where the elephant was located.

It seemed in a worse state than when Falconer had last seen it, its breath almost like a death rattle. The keeper was nowhere to be seen, and the beast's eyes spoke mournfully of abandonment. Disappointingly, Yeh-Lu was uninterested in the beast's condition, merely satisfying himself with having seen it.

'It is a poor example of its kind,' he murmured. 'I have seen people from the Indies and Kesimir fight from towers on elephants' backs as though they were in castles. They come from the lands where the Bakhshi live – those adept in necromancy and the diabolic arts.'

Falconer remembered that the Nestorian priest, David, had used the Latin word *baxitae* to describe those from whom Yeh-Lu had learned his magic tricks. These Bakhshi that Yeh-Lu mentioned were obviously one and the same. If they were necromancers, maybe they could have helped the elephant. It certainly seemed beyond human help now. Yeh-Lu wrinkled his nose at the stench in the barn and stared at the ray of sunlight as it cut across the foetid, straw-strewn floor. Suddenly he shook off his lethargy, and pulled the cloak tightly about him.

'I must return, or there will be questions asked about my absence.'

They left the sorry beast in peace, and Falconer showed

Yeh-Lu the way back to Carfax, where he might take North Gate Street to the town entrance opposite the Tartar encampment. Though he offered to accompany the man to the safety of the gate, Yeh-Lu insisted he could now make his own way, and didn't require Falconer at his side. Falconer put this down to a confidence bred of successful avoidance of discovery to date, and watched Yeh-Lu thread his inconspicuous way through the bustle of the food and corn markets that filled the colourful street. Soon he was lost in the crowd, and Falconer breathed a sigh of relief. But, just to be certain of his safety, he decided to observe the man's return to the Tartar camp.

He turned down Cheyney Lane, and emerged close by the steps that led up to the walkway atop the city walls. There he was not surprised to find Peter Bullock pacing the stone battlements. The constable had become obsessed by the brooding presence of the Tartars on his doorstep, and spent most of his time observing their actions. Or, as was more accurate, their lack of action. Today the camp was unusually quiet – not even the cocky figure of the commander was to be seen strutting around the large black tents that grew like pustules out of the green field. Bullock just grunted an acknowledgement at Falconer as he came up the steps, and returned his implacable gaze to the camp. Falconer went to stand next to him, leaning companionably on the warm yellow stones that topped the walls. He fumbled for his eye-lenses, looking left towards North Gate in order to spot Yeh-Lu's emergence from the city, and so he didn't see the start of the commotion down in the encampment.

'What's this?' muttered Bullock.

'What?' retorted Falconer, curious as to what Bullock might have seen, though he kept his lens-improved gaze on the stir of activity that was the entrance to Oxford. He spotted a heavily cloaked figure emerge, crossing the field in the general direction of the encampment, and was relieved. Yeh-Lu had not been spotted, and was making his inconspicuous way back to the camp.

Bullock grabbed his arm, almost causing him to drop his precious eye-lenses over the wall into the ditch below. 'Over in the Tartar camp. Something is very wrong down there.'

Falconer peered at the huddle of tents, and as the indistinct shapes sharpened into focus, he also heard some anguished cries carrying across to where he and Peter stood. One of the Tartar soldiers emerged from the smaller tent that stood somewhat aside from the two larger ones. Even at this distance, Falconer could tell that his sallow features were ashen. He called out something, and two more Tartars rushed into the tent. The tall, black figure of the Nestorian priest hovered nervously at some distance from the tent flap, as though afraid to enter. After a few moments the soldiers re-emerged, carrying a heavy bundle between them. When they laid it at the feet of the priest, Falconer could see it was a body. And as they lowered it to the ground, the head fell back, revealing a shock of spiky grey hair. It was the body of Noyan Chimbai.

Nine

For Guchuluk it had been a sleepless and busy night, so he had allowed himself the luxury of resting until the sun was high in the sky. As no one in the camp was eager to disturb him, he had not been apprised of Chimbai's unusual behaviour. The noyan had been left to do whatever he was doing in the little tent. But when, at last, Sigatay had been persuaded by David to investigate the mysterious and extended seclusion of Noyan Chimbai that fateful morning, the cries were enough to alert Guchuluk to the tragedy. He rushed out of his tent, pulling his light quilted jacket on as he ran. It was immediately obvious what the cause of the commotion was.

David's long, black form knelt at the side of the body, his hands clasped in prayer. The three soldiers – Sigatay, Khadakh and Achikh – stood sentinel over the scene. Achikh was too stupid to understand the trouble he was in, and just stared in bewilderment at the lifeless body. Khadakh, named after a legendary Tartar character whose sobriquet was 'The Valiant', did not at all resemble his namesake. The hand that held his bow was trembling, the knuckles white with tension. He knew he had failed in his duty – his only hope was that the worst of the punishment would fall on his superior. Sigatay, whose responsibility it was to secure the safety of the noyan, looked ashen, and was swaying slightly, as though he might collapse at any minute. At the sight of Chimbai's startled, but lifeless features, Guchuluk found it hard to suppress a smirk of satisfaction. He masked the uncontrollable grin by rubbing his stubbly chin, as if pondering what to do next.

'This will need some investigating, don't you think, Peter?'

Guchuluk looked up, startled by the sound of an unfamiliar tongue that he did not understand. Two men stood at a cautious and respectful distance from the group of Tartars. One was a bent, old man with heavy, muscular arms and a barrel of a chest. His clothes were old and patched, and a sword hung at his side. The old man's right hand hovered close to the sword's pommel, and Guchuluk recognized the stance of a soldier. The other man was tall, with a cropped thatch of grizzled hair. His black robe, too, had seen better years, and it did not hide the bear-like strength of the man. The aged man he didn't know, but he looked old enough to know Dua the One-eyed of ancient legend. Guchuluk recognized the other for one of the scholars who had been at the banquet earlier in the week. His name was something outlandish like Falknakh. Guchuluk snarled a command at the Nestorian priest:

'Tell them to go away.'

Nervously, David spoke to the two men in their own tongue, while Guchuluk stared at them through slitted eyes. The old man spoke first, and David looked relieved. He was about to translate what had been said for Guchuluk, when Falknakh interrupted, and the priest's face fell. He turned to protest, but Falknakh spoke again, more firmly this time. The old man at his side looked disconcerted, but was obviously used to deferring to the scholar's superiority.

'What is he saying?' asked Guchuluk suspiciously.

David cast his eyes to the ground, afraid to look straight at

Guchuluk as he spoke. 'The old man is the representative of law in the town, and was going to leave the death in our hands. But the other – you remember his name is Falconer—' David pronounced it without the gutturals with which Guchuluk had invested it. Guchuluk, a quick learner, muttered the correct pronunciation under his breath, and told the priest to get on.

'Falconer says he represents the King of England in such serious matters, and insists that he be allowed to examine the body.'

Guchuluk frowned. 'Could this be true?'

David shrugged his narrow shoulders. 'I have no way of knowing. But if it is true, we should not antagonize their king, bearing in mind our mission. And if it is false, what have we to lose? He may find out who killed the noyan for us.'

That thought didn't please Guchuluk, but he could not disagree with the priest. 'Let him do what he wishes, but keep an eye on him. It shall be your duty to ensure he does not pry where he is not wanted. Remember who is now in command.'

David understood immediately that Guchuluk was referring to himself, and told Falconer he could examine the body. The scholar came closer, and kneeled at Chimbai's side. He observed the feathers of an arrow protruding from the bloodstained mess of flesh, leather and quilting that was the Tartar commander's chest. Then he noticed that the body lay slightly twisted to one side, as if something prevented it from lying flat on the ground. Lifting the body with one hand, he felt the Noyan's back. He realized that under his tunic the tip and part of the shaft were poking out of Chimbai's back. Lifting the jacket carefully, he saw that the arrow was black with thick heart's blood, and marvelled at the deadly shot. The force of the arrow's flight had truly been great to rip through the tent in which Chimbai had been standing, and still drive on so far through the chest. And the accuracy of such a blind shot was a miracle.

He got to his feet, wiping the sticky blood off his fingers on to the long grass as he did so. Abruptly, Guchuluk pushed him aside, stooped over the body, and fumbled in the pocket of the commander's quilted jacket. After a moment of panic when he obviously couldn't find what he wanted, his fingers closed over what he was seeking. He drew out a small, oblong tablet of gold with a hole drilled in one end. It was a *paizah*, and whoever held it wielded the authority of the Great Khan himself. He held the object in his palm, and, wiping away the blood that stained the inscription, he read the legend out loud:

'By the strength of the great god, and of the great grace which he hath accorded to our emperor, may the name of the khan be blessed, and let all such as will not obey him be slain and be destroyed.'

'You are completely mad.' Bullock was still astounded at Falconer's audacity. 'That young Tartar . . .'

'Guchuluk.'

'Gutch-a-look. He looked as if he wanted to rip out your heart and eat it raw on the spot. And as for suggesting that you, of all people, are the legitimate representative of King Henry!' The constable's face was a bright crimson, such as Falconer had not seen since Bullock had got hopelessly drunk three Christmases ago, terrorizing the student population into observing the most subdued revels for many a year.

'It got us a look at the body, though, didn't it? And gave me enough authority in their eyes to ask a few questions.'

Bullock began to calm down, and had to grudgingly admit that Falconer was correct. Sitting now in the safety of the constable's chamber in St George's Tower, overlooking the castle walls, he could feel relief that Falconer's masquerade had not ended more seriously. It might have gone badly wrong for both of them. But now he, too, was consumed with curiosity about the interrogations the scholar had conducted through the agency of the Tartar priest. 'And what did you learn from all your questions?'

'That Chimbai must have died between sunrise and the middle of the day – say between prime and terce. I can be no more accurate than that because the guards were too afraid to disturb him. But no one could have been in close proximity to the body when he died. The three members of Chimbai's bodyguard could see all sides of the tent and the ground around it. And you could see for yourself that there was nothing but open land all around. It would have been impossible for anyone to sneak up, shoot an arrow in the noyan, and sneak away without being seen.'

'The bodyguards could have been inattentive. Many sentries are – and I speak from personal experience.'

Falconer couldn't imagine Bullock having shirked his responsibilities as a sentry in his younger days in Henry's army. 'I doubt they were careless. You could see from their looks that they were petrified about what had happened. I would bet that their attention to duty is based on a stark fear of the consequences of failure. No, the murderer didn't enter the tent while they were on guard.'

'Then he must have secreted himself in the tent before the commander and his guards arrived.' Bullock was sure this could be the only logical conclusion. But still Falconer did not fully agree.

'Possibly. But, if he did, where was he when the men finally entered the tent to find the noyan dead? All insist that, when they burst in, the tent was empty save for the effigies of their gods. And the body.'

'Could someone have been hiding, only to sneak away during the confusion over the body's discovery?'

Falconer pursed his lips and frowned. 'It's possible. But that speaks of a risky and desperate strategy, when everything else suggests a well-planned manœuvre. No, the arrow must have been shot from outside the tent.'

Bullock snorted in derision. 'A fantastically lucky shot – to pierce the heart without a clear sight of the man. You might as well suggest that his god fired the arrow.' The constable meant it as a joke, but Falconer went along with him, nodding as if seriously considering the option.

'Hmm – a lightning bolt from the gods. Unfortunately, it was a very worldly arrow I saw sticking out of his chest. But I would not rule out anything at this stage – even magic.'

Later, he was to regret bringing that word into the investigation – even in jest. But for the moment it was forgotten as another, more fantastic but sickening possibility entered his head. Until now, he had discarded the dark words spoken by Nicholas de Ewelme, Chancellor of the University, as they had left the unsuccessful first meeting with the Tartars. Now they reverberated around his skull again as he strove to find a culprit for the murder. What was it precisely de Ewelme had said – 'Something will have to be done about these monsters?'

'Just what I said all along,' muttered Bullock truculently, making Falconer realize he had repeated the chancellor's threat out loud.

'No, no. Someone said that to me only a few days ago, and now one of the "monsters" is dead.' Falconer put up a warning hand to stop Bullock's questioning look. 'I am not going to tell you who it was – it would be safer for you not to know. If he is the killer, I might be his next victim. And you, too, if he fears discovery as much as I think he would.'

But could the pale, scrawny milksop of a chancellor really have fired the shot that killed Chimbai? Not himself, assuredly. But he was capable of employing others to carry out the deed – a student at the university, perhaps. He would have to ask his own students at Aristotle's Hall if they knew of a marksman capable of shooting such a shaft as struck the Tartar commander down. In the meantime, he must arrange to get a look at the tent in which the deed was done. Guchuluk had expressly forbidden this earlier – indeed the young commander had been markedly reluctant to allow Falconer to interfere at all. It appeared he did not want anyone prying into how the commander had died. But it was vital to Falconer's understanding of the murder to see the interior of the tent where the body had been found. Either the arrow was shot through the opening in the tent, or through the tent wall itself, and a rent in the covering would tell him where the marksman had stood.

While Bullock fussed around in his little larder, returning to its cool shelf the jug of ale that had accompanied the simple midday meal of pottage the two men had shared, Falconer suddenly had an idea. If he could somehow enlist the support of Yeh-Lu, he might be able to gain access to the tent where the murder took place. After he had set in train the search for a miraculous student archer, he would go to the camp and speak to Yeh-Lu. He quickly rose from his seat, and, calling out his thanks for the repast to his friend, left for Aristotle's Hall. Bullock emerged from the larder, once again cursing that he had just remembered to tell Falconer of Guillaume de Beaujeu's lurking presence in Oxford only to have his friend disappear on him.

As Sir Hugh Leyghton rode into Oxford through North Gate, he noticed the abrupt change in fortunes of the shop-keepers lining the street. When he had left a few days earlier, the proximity of the monstrous Tartar emcampment had depressed the area so much that only a few inhabitants ventured to the stalls nearest the gate. Vegetables had lain rotting on the trestles, and scrawny chickens poked their heads disconsolately through the bars of their cages as their sellers pondered the cost of continuing to feed them.

Now the whole market was full of people and buzzing with rumour. The corn merchants had abandoned their stalls and stood in a huddle in the centre of the street, a look of glee written on all their faces. They were so excited as to ignore Sir Hugh's peremptory calls to clear the way, and he was forced to take his charger over the stinking sewage channel in the middle of the street, risking laming the creature on the uneven gully. Beyond the corn merchants, other knots of traders were eagerly swapping news with each other across their trestles. Their voices carried to Sir Hugh, and now the full import of what had roused everyone came to him.

'The Lord has struck down Gog . . .'

'One of the Tartars had been killed . . .'

'. . . by his own graven effigy . . .'

'They say the whole encampment will be destroyed.'

This last came from a wall-eyed fishmonger, who did his trade no good by the comment, because all his customers, on hearing the rumour, raced for the city walls and a view of the devastation. Sir Hugh recovered his good humour at the story that was circulating, and spurred his horse in the direction of South Gate, and Bernard de Genova's friary. What he and the Dominican had spoken about only a few days ago had come about, it appeared. And he was anxious to get the full story from Bernard. The only jarring element of what was becoming a very pleasant day came as he crossed the busy thoroughfare of Carfax. There, the conflux of people crossing from wood-

merchant to glove-maker, tannery to bread stall, pig market
to potter, created a jam of bodies that even a nobleman on
horseback had difficulty negotiating. Spotting a gap in the ebb
and flow, Sir Hugh twisted the bridle on his charger to turn
the horse's head, and thread his way through.

Suddenly a shabbily clad peasant strode out of the crowd
and almost under the horse's neck, causing Sir Hugh to pull
sharply on his reins. The man stumbled to one side, and, as he
did so, grabbed the horse's ornate bridle to steady himself. Sir
Hugh raised his gloved hand to strike the impudent fellow,
but the man look up, unafraid, straight into Leyghton's eyes.
Somehow, the blow never fell, and the curse that was to
accompany it died on Leyghton's lips. He wrenched on the
bridle, and the man released it, disappearing back into the
throng, leaving Sir Hugh Leyghton wondering why Guillaume
de Beaujeu, Knight Templar, was scurrying around Oxford
dressed like a peasant.

The encounter was so odd that by the time he reached the
Dominican friary at Trill Mill, he was beginning to wonder if
he had dreamed it. Perhaps the man had just resembled the
Templar; indeed it was some twenty-five years or more since
he had last seen de Beaujeu. It had been when both had been
youths, and the Frenchman had been with a party of Templars
bringing the news of Geoffrey Leyghton's death to his parents.
Hugh had been ushered into an ante-room by one of the
servants, so that Sir Thomas Leyghton and his wife could hear
the stark and tragic news of the loss of their favoured, eldest
son in private. Whilst in France, Geoffrey's Templar order
had summoned him to the defence of Christendom, when
news of the Tartar invasion filtered through to the Western
world around 1240. A year later, at Leignitz, a massed army
of Templars, Hospitallers, Teutonic Knights and mercenaries
under the command of Henry of Silesia was routed by the

stocky little men on horseback. The Templar force was totally lost, and Geoffrey's comrades came to tell his parents of their loss. Amongst the contingent had been the young, devout Guillaume. Even then, de Beaujeu's eyes had been cold and frightening, and Sir High was sure the self-same eyes had stayed his angry blow just now in the square.

He dismounted in the inner courtyard of the friary, and sent one of its Preacher inmates to announce his presence to Adam Grasse.

'And tell him I wish permission to talk to Brother Bernard.'

Though he was anxious to speak to Bernard de Genova, he would observe the proper amenities first. As ambassador for the king, he would ensure the senior Dominican's nose was not put out of joint, before glorying in the demise of the Tartar with Brother Bernard. He itched to know how the friar had achieved their objective, and so soon. The Preacher friar who stood before him gave him a strange look, but went on his errand.

An unconscionable time passed, with Sir Hugh pacing impatiently round the cloister, becoming increasingly annoyed at the lack of prompt attention. Gradually he became aware that his presence had not caused the usual stir in the friary. The Dominicans were normally a nosy bunch, who would have found any excuse to pass by and attempt to discover the purpose of his visit. By now he should have been 'accidentally' encountered by a number of friars. In fact, it suddenly dawned on him that the cloister was unusually silent.

Then the Preacher whom he had sent for Brother Adam reappeared, a grim look on his face. He asked politely if Leyghton would accompany him, then turned away abruptly, apparently expecting no objection. Like an acolyte at his initiation, the perplexed Sir Hugh followed the friar, as his sandalled feet slapped on the cold cloister slabs. The

Preacher eventually ushered him through a door into a small, gloomy cell, and retreated. At first Leyghton thought he had been left alone, and could not imagine this cramped and chilly environment was the office of Adam Grasse. But when his eyes, accustomed to the glare of the midday sun, adjusted to the darkness, he realized that Grasse was indeed standing in the darkest corner of the cell. The friar's voice, when he spoke, carried an edge of coldness that chilled Sir Hugh Leyghton even more than the atmosphere of the cell had done.

'This is Brother Bernard's cell. But I'm afraid he is not here at the present.'

Sir Hugh did not understand the import of the friar's statement. 'Then, if I may, I will await his return. I need to speak to him concerning an urgent matter about the Tartar embassy.'

'Then you may have a long wait.' In response to Leyghton's puzzled look, Grasse waddled over to the simple bed in the corner of the cell and dramatically threw the cover back.

Sir Hugh sucked in his breath at the sight of the bloodstain. 'Where is Bernard?'

Grasse shrugged. 'I was hoping you could tell me that.'

The Tartar camp appeared deserted as Falconer approached it across the open meadow, where the colourful summer flowers belied the sombre mood that hung over the little group of tents. He wondered if the occupants of the black tents had stolen away in the night, as silently as they had come. But when he got as far as the two scorched marks on the earth where the burning torches had blazed on that first night, the flap of the main tent opened, and Yeh-Lu emerged. His eyes scanned Falconer, and he nodded imperceptibly, but then turned back inside the tent.

It was the priest, David, who emerged next, and scurried over to where Falconer stood. With his shaky Latin and a smattering of English, he enquired of Falconer what he wanted. It took Falconer several minutes before he made the priest understand he wanted to examine the tent in which the body had been found. At one point, when David seemed wilfully to misunderstand him, he almost called for Yeh-Lu. But then he thought that the Oriental might not wish it known that he spoke the language of the English, nor perhaps that he ventured out on his own into Oxford and communicated with a Franciscan friar. Finally the Nestorian nodded his comprehension, and disappeared into the tent. Again there was silence, and Falconer's eyes strayed to the object of his request. The small tent, like the others, had an opening that faced south, towards the city walls. The flap at the entrance was now open, tied back with cord. Had it been so when the noyan had been inside, affording an archer a view of him? Falconer couldn't remember. One thing he was certain of, though. When he had observed the encampment from Oxford's walls, he was sure that one of the Tartar commander's bodyguard had stood in line with the opening and the walls. Unless the guard himself had fired the fatal arrow, it would have been difficult to shoot the commander through the opening. It only remained to discover whether there was a tear in the back of the tent where the arrow might have pierced it. He was starting to walk towards the little tent when David reappeared. The priest was startled to see that Falconer had moved, and hurried over to where the scholar now stood. Taking him firmly by the arm, he led him back to the main tent, glancing in fear back at the smaller one.

'Chimbai – he is in the sacred tent. You cannot go in.'

'But I must see the site of the crime – as the king's representative, it is essential I do so.'

David grimaced. 'Then maybe tomorrow. Yes – tomorrow, I will arrange it.'

Falconer stared the priest in the eye, trying to ascertain if he or someone else in the camp had something to hide by the manœuvre. David's eyes dropped to the ground, and he shuffled his feet on the dry, dusty earth.

'Then, in that case, I will speak to everyone again. And you will help me.'

With that, Falconer bent down and pushed through the tent flap. Surprisingly, Yeh-Lu was the only one inside, and he sat impassively on the raised dais where Falconer had last seen the Tartar commander alive. A quizzical look crossed his features, and he made a point of addressing David in the guttural Tartar tongue. He obviously wasn't going to speak English to Falconer, or admit any further acquaintance beyond that on the night of the banquet. David translated what Yeh-Lu had said for Falconer's benefit.

'He says – what more do you want?'

Falconer ignored the question. 'Where are the others?'

'Others?'

'Guchuluk and the bodyguard.'

David smiled weakly. 'They are in the other tent – Guchuluk's tent. He is in charge now, and we are excluded from the . . . military decisions.'

It suddenly occurred to Falconer that, when David had ducked back into the tent the first time, he could only have been conferring with Yeh-Lu about his request to see what they called the 'sacred tent'. It had been Yeh-Lu, then, not Guchuluk, who had put Falconer off until the following day. Bearing that in mind, he continued the charade of speaking to Yeh-Lu through the agency of the Nestorian.

'Do you or Yeh-Lu know of anyone who had a reason to kill the noyan?'

The priest paled, but shook his head vigorously.

'And Yeh-Lu?'

David looked puzzled, but Falconer persisted. 'Tell him what I said — does he know of anyone with reason to kill Chimbai?'

David reluctantly did so, and Yeh-Lu laughed, and answered with a single word.

'What did he say?'

The priest blushed, and mumbled, 'Everyone.'

Falconer was exasperated at Yeh-Lu's obtuseness, and almost started to question him direct. Perhaps realizing what might happen, Yeh-Lu spoke again to David, though his eyes never left Falconer. The priest clearly did not want to translate what was said, and shot a reply back. His whining tones didn't impress Yeh-Lu, however, who waved a peremptory hand at David. Reluctantly, the priest spoke for the other man, fear in his eyes.

'He says there is someone here who was particularly adverse to how Chimbai ran matters.'

Yeh-Lu spoke in the guttural tongue again, obviously urging David on.

'He says that one man had good reason to kill Chimbai . . .' He still hesitated to say the word, but Yeh-Lu's look cowed him into submission. But before he could utter the name, he had to qualify it with his own statement. Quietly, but insistently, he warned Falconer, 'You must realize that Yeh-Lu is not a Mongol. He is from a subject race who do not have the same sense of loyalty.'

Falconer smiled inwardly, knowing Yeh-Lu understood everything that David was saying about him, and nodded. 'Yes, but who is he talking about?'

David grimaced, and whispered the name: 'Guchuluk.'

*

Miles Bikerdyke waited outside the chancellor's quarters, nervously glancing over his shoulder, and picking the head off the boil on his neck. The student would have preferred not to have been seen in Nicholas de Ewelme's doorway, but when he had knocked to gain admittance, the ancient servant who opened the door had asked his business, then slammed the oaken door in his face whilst he carried the youth's message to his master. Halegod – no one knew his first name – had been servant to the chancellors of Oxford University for nigh on fifty years. He was long past being able to cope with his duties, but no chancellor, least of all de Ewelme, had had the courage to dispense with his services. So the ancient roamed the halls of the chancellor's residence, and interfered with the smooth running of the establishment at every opportunity. His firmest maxim was that no student should be allowed into the house – especially so after one chancellor, Thomas de Cantilupe, had been almost split in two by a drunken student's sword during a brawl. The fact that nothing worse than a tear to the hem of de Cantilupe's ceremonial robe had resulted, hadn't changed his mind.

Miles was on the verge of fleeing from his prominent position in the chancellor's doorway when the door was flung open, and de Ewelme himself pulled the youth inside. The redoubtable Halegod could be seen scurrying to the rear of the house, clucking his disapproval at the chancellor's rash act. De Ewelme slammed the door behind them both, then, as if he had run out of decisiveness, hovered uncertainly in the gloomy passage that ran from the front door of the house to the rear. Miles Bikerdyke rubbed his boil in embarrassment. Finally the older man spoke up:

'It is done, then?'

Miles nodded, and grinned. 'It was easy, I just had to be in the right place at the right time, and . . .'

De Ewelme held his hands up in horror, staving off the youth's flow of words. 'Please — the less I know about your actions the better.' He thrust a bag of chinking coins into the youth's hand. 'It is sufficient that they have been successful.'

Ten

*I will set fire on Magog and on those who live undisturbed
in the coasts and islands, and they shall know I am the Lord.*

Ezekiel 39:6

Sometimes, Falconer found the little enclosed world of
scholarship quite stifling. He longed for the fresh air and
wide vistas of sea travel, and the excited anticipation of arrival
at an unfamiliar destination. At one time in his youth each
great city on the northern waterway of Europe had been new
to him. Paris, Bruges, Augsburg, Prague and Cracow had all
seemed outlandish, slowly opening up their secrets to him.
Then, travels with merchants had brought him to Naples,
Barcelona and Marseilles, through which flowed oil, wine, rice
and grain from the edges of the world scattered around the
Mediterranean Sea. From there he had gone to the source of
those products, until one day he had suddenly felt a yearning
to return to England. Not that he was jaded by the extraordi-
nary sights he had seen for the last ten years. He simply had
had a feeling that he would make greater sense of what he had
seen from the perspective of his own country. He would have
explained it to his students now in this way. Having filled
himself with knowledge *per experientiam propriam* – from his
own experience – he needed to seek the causes, and demon-
strate *propter quid* – why things were so. But lately he had
become tired with the quibbles demonstrating why such-and-
such was so-and-so. Why not just lie back, accept that it was
so, and enjoy the world?

He sighed, and thought of his friend, Roger Bacon, closeted in his tower, trying to define the world in a vast treatise, and failing to involve himself in its reality. He had gone straight from the Tartar encampment across the city to Bacon's tower. He had hoped for some assistance with his investigations, and perhaps a revival of his old friendship, only to be confronted by a distraught and pale-faced old man. Bacon had, for once, allowed Falconer into his chamber, and the scholar had been astonished at how, in the few days that the Franciscan had been resident, the room had accumulated a chaotic collection of strange items and documents. It was as if the room and its occupant had attracted all the unusual detritus floating around Oxford for the ten years that Bacon had been absent. Large tomes that the friar could not have brought in his small satchel had been piled on the single table, and more were stacked on the floor. Several glass alembics stood in one corner, some half-full of noxious-looking liquids. One had been dropped, and its contents oozed from the spidery network of cracks into the chipped and scarred floorboards. Strangely shaped pieces of wood and metal lay in profusion everywhere.

It was no surprise to Falconer, therefore, that the distracted Bacon, after letting him in, had wandered round the room, muttering, 'It is lost. It is lost.' Falconer had attempted to help him, but the conversation had gone from bad to worse.

'It is lost.'

'What is lost?'

'I cannot say.'

'But, if you do not know what it is that is lost, how do you know it is lost?'

'No, no, William. You do not take my meaning. I cannot yet tell you what it is that is lost.'

The irritable Bacon continued to rummage around the piles of jars, metal shapes that took the form of wheels with spikes, and weighty cylinders. Falconer suddenly felt ignored, not only at that moment but from the day that Bacon had returned to Oxford. He must have had contact with other scholars – where would he have got all this clutter otherwise? – but he had not seen fit to talk to his oldest friend. Clearly the friendship had not survived its ten-year hiatus, and would not be restored. Aggrieved, he left the friar to his search, and crept down the spiral stairs, and through the stinking skinner's yard below.

Now, full of gloom, and not sure that he wanted to continue the investigation into Chimbai's death, he returned to Aristotle's Hall. Like his heart, it, too, was empty and cold, and he climbed the staircase up to his solar in the highest part of the building.

Before he could raise the latch on the door, he heard the low murmur of a familiar voice. Opening the door, he saw Ann Segrim sitting at his table, with the normally aloof Balthazar perched on her wrist, enjoying a caressing finger on his downy head. The owl's big eyes were closed, and Falconer envied him Ann's gentle touch. As he closed the door, he wondered if anyone in the hall had seen the woman's arrival. The concern must have shown on his face, for Ann grinned.

'Fear not, no one saw me come. And if we take care, no one will see me go.'

Balthazar opened his eyes at the cessation of Ann's caresses, and cast a baleful look at his master. With a hop and a disdainful flap of his silent wings, he retreated to his perch in the far corner of the room. Falconer's mood still enveloped him, and so Ann continued:

'I came to market with Humphrey's steward, Sekston, so I thought I would take the opportunity to seek you out.'

'I am honoured.' Falconer had not meant the words to

sound tart, but they did, so he quickly added, 'Where is he now?'

'I gave him a coin to spend at his favourite tavern, but it will not last him, so I cannot be long.' She paused, as if embarrassed to explain her reason for calling. Then she took a deep breath and began. 'I went to see the elephant. The poor thing is near death, as far as I can see. And its keeper has all but abandoned it. I saw him drinking in the same tavern that Sekston entered. What can we do to save it?'

Falconer pulled a face — the demise of the great beast was the least of his worries. So he replied in a rather offhand manner.

'We can do nothing — the beast's way of life is unknown to us.'

Ann's whole body stiffened, shocked that the man she trusted and admired could be so uncaring — and unscientific. She pushed herself up from her seat and swept over to the door. 'Then we should learn about it. If we understood its life, and didn't repeat stupid legends about it — 'her face reddened, but she spat the word out — 'copulating back-to-back, we might be able to save its life.'

With that, she stormed out, leaving the perplexed Falconer wondering if his tutelage was still required.

Guchuluk was angry. Having expressly forbidden the interfering Falconer from the camp, he had emerged from his yurt early in the afternoon to see the man returning to the city's North Gate. The look on David's face was enough to tell him that Falconer had been poking his nose in where it was not wanted. He had grabbed the priest by the collar of his greasy black robe and pushed him back into the yurt. With Yeh-Lu looking on in amusement, he had squeezed the truth out of

David – Falconer wanted to see the yurt where the murder had taken place, and the fool priest had agreed to his demand. Guchuluk could not believe it – the Englishman would be wanting to interrogate him next. And that he could not have.

He had only just finished scaring Sigatay and his confederates into submission, and now it seemed likely he would have to do the same with the two civilian members of the embassy. The soldiers had been easy to scare: he simply had to threaten them with death for their dereliction of duty as regards Chimbai. Their fear would ensure absolute loyalty to the new commander. David and Yeh-Lu would be a little more difficult to handle, the latter especially, because Guchuluk could not fathom the man from the city of Cambaluc. He was as devious as most of his race, and Guchuluk knew a livelier mind operated behind the subservient mask than was shown in his role as administrator. But at least he had no reason to be in contact with the English, and could not speak their outlandish tongue.

The priest, on the other hand, was required to act as interpreter, and therefore was in constant intercourse with the locals. This position, and his unfortunate inability to control his tongue, made him a volatile and dangerous tool, who could give away secrets about Guchuluk that he would prefer kept dark. On reflection, Guchuluk decided, David was the more problematic of the two men in his party, and resolved to keep a close eye on him. If necessary, he would have to be dealt with swiftly and finally. In the mean time, he had to plan for the consequences of Chimbai's murder.

Darkness can hide many sins, and though Oxford appeared quiet that night, Peter Bullock knew that it was an illusion created by the soft, all-enveloping gloom. There was much happening under cover of darkness that the perpetrators would not undertake in daylight. In Torold's Lane, not far from where Guillaume de Beaujeu had lodgings, a night-stalker robbed a drunken and unwary sheep farmer of his purse, hamstringing him with a dagger in the process. The sheep farmer was never to walk properly again. A regent master of divinity, Ralph Wyght, paid the first of many nocturnal visits to a tailor's wife, her husband having been despatched on a fruitless overnight errand. His foolish dalliance would eventually bring him before the Chancellor's Court, to be censured by his peers. One of Nicholas de Ewelme's servants lost all his money dicing at the Cardinal's Hat tavern with a motley crew of travellers who professed to have just met each other. Under cover of the same darkness, those travellers moved on together to find a gullible mark in Banbury. By comparison, the fire was a trivial matter to each of these people. Especially as it was in the Tartar camp.

Peter Bullock saw it first, from the top of the city walls. He had just finished getting the facts of the robbery from the bleeding sheep farmer, and had got him carried off to St John's Hospital outside East Gate. The friars would tend to him there, but the leg wound was vicious and deep, and Peter doubted if he would walk without a limp. He had finally convinced all the on-lookers hanging out of their windows that there was nothing more to see, and that the king's peace had been re-established. With all the shutters reluctantly closed, and dust scuffed over the dark bloodstain in the lane, he returned to his nocturnal observation of the Tartars. He knew it was foolish – knew that they presented no military threat – but he could not tear himself away. It wasn't even as though there was anything to see, as the camp was usually as dead as King Henry's father.

Tonight was no different, and he was on the verge of giving up his vigil for the night when he thought he did see some movement. He cursed his old eyes, and screwed his face up to see better in the gloom. There was nothing, and he assumed it must have been his imagination, or at most a stray dog looking for scraps. Then he was sure he saw a light flicker and disappear, and wondered if someone were wandering around the camp with a burning torch. Suddenly the flame appeared again – this time more distinct. There was somebody abroad in the camp – he could see a black figure outlined by the now steady glow. Then flames shot up into the night sky, illuminating the tents around it. And Bullock could see that the source of the flames was one of the tents itself – the small one where the noyan's body lay. With an audible roar, the side of the tent was engulfed in flame, and sparks flew up into the sky, drifting dangerously close to the tinder-dry hovels along St Giles.

For a moment the constable stood with his mouth agape, then, realizing the danger to the town, he scuttled down the steps into Sumnor's Lane and burst into the silent church of St Michael. The bell rope hung down from the blackness of the tower, and he grabbed it, yanking it ferociously. At first the heavy bell swung in infuriating silence, then the clapper hit the bell, and the alarm was raised.

Falconer stood disconsolately on the edge of the blackened grass. The stench of burning still hung heavy in the air, along with the whitish smoke that drifted lazily from the remains of the noyan's last resting place. The tent was no more than a skeleton of half-burned poles, poking into the red dawn sky. The covering of felt, soaked in pitch to shed the rain, had burned away completely – as had most of the contents of the tent, including the noyan's body. The ash was still hot, and Falconer could approach no further than the circle burned on the earth. There was no hope now that he could examine the tent and discover where the arrow had been fired from. All the evidence had literally gone up in smoke. More in resignation than expectation, he fumbled in his pouch and held his eye-lenses up. In the mass of charred remains at the centre of the pyre, all he could see was the white of some bones, and the greyish leftovers of some metal – weapons or armour, presumably. The heat at the core of the fire began to scorch his face, and he pulled back, pocketing his lenses.

No one from Oxford, roused by St Michael's church bell, had bothered with the seat of the fire. It was the sparks flying into the night sky, threatening the huddle of the thatched and largely wooden houses on St Giles, that had occupied the citizenry. As one large cinder after another floated down from above, people beat out the incipient fires with brooms and bare hands. The occasional bucket of water taken from the moat surrounding the castle and passed along a chain of hands also helped to save the quarter. Only one man had died, falling from the roof as he tried to pull his smouldering thatch down. Left to their own devices with an already raging fire to tackle, Guchuluk's entourage could only stand and stare as Chimbai's impromptu funeral pyre blazed. Of Guchuluk himself, there had been no sign.

Glumly, Falconer felt that this was a murder investigation that had ended before it had ever begun. He had had no more than a brief glimpse of the corpse before it had been burned beyond recognition, and the scene of the crime, and any clues it held, had been reduced to ashes. Even the murdered noyan's countrymen didn't want him to pry into the killing. What facts did he have to apply his logic to in order to deduce the greater truth – the identity of the murderer? Chimbai had apparently been killed by an arrow shot by an excellent marksman, between the hours of prime and sext, while surrounded by guards who saw nothing. According to rumour, more than one person had wanted him dead. Nicholas de Ewelme had certainly threatened dire action, and Yeh-Lu said there was friction between the noyan and his second-in-command. Precious few facts to develop a scientific theory on. But, for now, Guchuluk must remain the primary suspect, especially as he was conspicuously absent, and may have set the fire himself to destroy evidence.

A nervous cough behind him alerted Falconer to someone else's presence at the site of the conflagration. It was the Nestorian priest. He clearly had something to say, though, as he shifted from one foot to the other and picked at the frayed edge of his sleeve, he was having some difficulty in coming out with it. Falconer wondered if what he had to say was going to be crucial – would it finally give him a way into this frustrating investigation? but when David spoke, it was of Yeh-Lu, and must have been based on envy of the other man's position. He said he didn't want Falconer to take Yeh-Lu's words about Guchuluk being Chimbai's nemesis at face value.

'The man has jealousies and hatreds of his own. And he is capable of magic – you saw it for yourself, when he made the cups fly, and cut himself to pieces up the rope, only to reappear whole. Why, I wouldn't put it past him to have murdered my Lord Chimbai himself.'

Falconer snorted. He didn't believe in magic, and knew that Yeh-Lu's tricks were effected by sleight-of-hand. Startling and mystifying they were, but in the end nothing more than illusions. Anyway, Yeh-Lu would truly have had to have been a necromancer to have killed Chimbai, because it would have required him to be in two places at once. The one fact that Falconer was sure of was that when Chimbai was being shot with bow and arrow Yeh-Lu had been in his own company. David's envy, and Yeh-Lu's secretiveness, did, however, assist him in their own way. If David were so keen to blame the innocent Yeh-Lu, whom he couldn't have known was with Falconer at the time of the murder, then what was he himself trying to conceal?

It could yet prove useful that the priest was his only way of communicating with the Tartar party. His constant presence while interrogating the others could be a way of verifying David's truthfulness and whereabouts during the murder and the fire-raising. He grasped David's arm firmly, and felt the man flinch.

'Come. I must speak with Guchuluk, and you must translate.'

David paled, and stammered over pronouncing the name of his new master. 'Guch-Guch-uluk?'

'What's the matter? Are you afraid of what he might say?'

David, who knew Guchuluk was not in the camp, and feared that he might not want it known, anxiously cast about for an excuse to give to this persistent Englishman.

'By Tengri, if you were a bahadur of my obok, then you would be dead by now.'

Guchuluk's voice was chilling, and David stiffened at its sound, thanking God that he was not a knight in the Mangkhut clan. He was a Kerait Mongol – his ancestors had betrayed the great Chinghis, and were still made to pay for it by those of the royal household. That was why he was here – as their eyes and ears. But David was not a born spy, and the unexpected return of Guchuluk caused him to break out into a sweat, and his heart to feel sick.

Falconer took note of this exchange, and though he understood not a word, he could guess what was being said by the young warrior. The priest was clearly frightened – his face was green and clammy – but Falconer could discern something about Guchuluk that David couldn't, scared as he was. The young man was trying to maintain a haughty air, but there was a shiftiness about his eyes that Falconer, used to the guilt of erring youths, could easily see. Where had he been when the fire had been set? Was his unease to do with the fact that the figure Bullock had seen near the tent before it went up in flames was Guchuluk himself? Falconer took a decision.

'David, translate for me. Ask Guchuluk where he was when the fire broke out.'

Sir Hugh Leyghton had a problem. The king had not been able to make his mind up about the Tartar envoys. One moment Henry was swayed by his son, Edward, who saw advantage for crusading in the Holy Land if the Tartars were persuaded to enter on the side of the Christian armies. The next moment he told Sir Hugh to prevaricate, recalling that it was but eight years since Pope Alexander had excommunicated the Count Bohemund for creating an alliance with the Tartars. Finally, Sir Hugh, himself filled with a crushing hatred of the Tartars, had been pleased to leave the court at Shrewsbury, ordered to talk and nothing else – in effect to string the Tartars along, but give them nothing. It was only on the third day of his return journey, just short of Witney, that he had been overtaken by a messenger bearing a sealed note.

Perplexed, the knight had taken it, and as he broke the seal and read the contents, the messenger rode off whence he had come. The letter urged Sir Hugh to cobble together some sort of agreement with the Tartars that could be used in the future – he could promise any level of armed provision he chose, as, like any pact, it was unlikely to be honoured. The message was clearly in Prince Edward's hand, but it was unsigned, and therefore deniable. Sir Hugh had sighed deeply, and wished for the guidance of his brother, Geoffrey, who he felt sure would have known what to do. Hugh constantly tried to match himself against his saintly brother, but knew he was always doomed to fail. He had schooled himself in the knightly skills, proud as his scrawny child's body had developed into the powerful weapon it now was. But, try as he might, he always felt dwarfed by Geoffrey, whose intellect matched his physical stature. Presented with a knotty problem, Hugh was always tempted to use his strength to cut through it. And that always seemed to go wrong. Geoffrey also had one great advantage over him – he would never grow old, nor have his reputation sullied.

Now, back in Oxford, and trapped between the Scylla and Charybdis of royal father and son, Sir Hugh Leyghton had walked straight into the mystery of Bernard's disappearance. Well, a mystery to Brother Adam Grasse anyway. If what Leyghton suspected were true, the friar was hiding because of the bloody deed in which Sir Hugh himself had played no small part. If the friar had carried on as normal, no suspicion would have been attracted towards him – or Sir Hugh. But instead he had left a bloodied bed as evidence, and gone into hiding, precisely as though he had something to conceal. Sir Hugh's conversation with the friar immediately after the disastrous Tartar feast had gone seriously awry, and he was not about to be dragged down with the fool. He stared in frustration at the blank walls of his lodgings as if expecting de Genova to materialize before him. The guest house in the Trill Mill friary was small and depressing, making no allowances for the opulent lifestyle to which Sir Hugh was accustomed. He began to pace the miserable cell, and pondered his next action.

'And Gutch-a-look stormed off without answering your question!' Bullock roared with laughter. 'Are you surprised?'

Falconer grinned self-consciously. 'No really. But, if he had replied, I would have something more to add to my paltry collection of facts. And, besides, he was so full of his own importance, I just had to annoy him.'

The two men sat in Bullock's chamber high in the castle keep, sopping up with their trencher bread the gravy of stew provided by the mistress of the Golden Ball Inn. The room was spartan where Falconer's was cluttered; clean and neat where Falconer's was dusty and smelling of owl droppings. It betrayed Bullock's life as a foot soldier in the interminable skirmishes that raged back and forth across the baronies of England, and over the sea in France, Aquitaine, Burgundy, and any number of other petty fiefdoms deemed worth fighting over. That he had survived into old age was testimony to Bullock's fighting skill, given that the infantry were mere fodder for soaking up the strength of the enemy, before the gallant knights on horseback safely entered the fray. Bullock would deprecate any suggestion that skill was involved, however – merely guile and a knack for self-preservation. Now his fighting days were over, he would not have liked to incur the wrath of a Tartar. Still, he chortled at the thought.

'These inhuman creatures have decimated the might of the West's armies, and savaged Templar knights by the score. They have employed suicide tactics to draw men into traps, and deflowered innocent maidens and sliced off their lily-white breasts as food for their overlord . . .'

Falconer had to intervene. 'Now, we do not know that is true.'

But Bullock was not to be stopped in his amused summation of the Tartars' evils. 'They ate the old and ugly women – though I dare say that was a mercy – and drank mares' blood. They are reckoned at a thousand thousand in number. And Regent Master William Falconer has the temerity to poke this wild beast with a meteorical pike.' He raised his mug in mock salute, slopping dregs of beer across his well-scrubbed table.

Falconer, knowing that the constable meant metaphorical, but not caring to correct him, dropped his head in amused acknowledgement. Then, suddenly, he looked up at Bullock. The spark of a thought had entered his ale-fuddled head, and almost extinguished itself immediately. He squeezed his eyes closed in an attempt to keep it alight.

'Suicide tactics?'

'Yes. They'd send a troop of horsemen into the centre of a battle. They would appear to be weakened, and turn tail. Our bold knights would give chase, and fall into a trap from which they could not escape. A killing ground of arrows.' Bullock shivered at the vision he had conjured up, and suddenly felt sober. He narrowed his eyes, and peered at Falconer. 'Why do you want to know?'

Falconer shook his head, because he didn't quite know himself. But there was some connection to Guchuluk there, and he would fit it together eventually. In the mean time, he would get Bullock to help him keep an eye on the new Tartar commander. 'If you see our mutual friend sneaking about, while you are on your nightly vigil on the walls, perhaps you could follow him.'

Bullock grunted in disbelief. 'No Tartar has entered this city, day or night. Nor ever will.'

Falconer thought of Yeh-Lu's clandestine journeys to the hovels outside the walls, and his own complicity in whisking him undiscovered from South Gate to North Gate. 'I am sure you are right. But if you do see any activity, let me know.'

Bullock nodded, then, still a little drunk, leaned forward, beckoning Falconer closer with a beefy finger. 'I can tell you of some clandestine activity that is already taking place within the city. A certain Templar of our acquaintance has been here for days without revealing himself to anyone. He's staying at that hovel of an inn in Torold's Lane. Which is cause for great suspicion in itself.'

Falconer, surprised at this revelation, cut the constable off in mid-flow: 'Guillaume de Beaujeu, in Oxford now? Peter — why didn't you tell me sooner?' Falconer shot up from the table, tipping his stool over behind him. The startled Bullock jerked backwards and almost toppled from his own perch. His ale mug landed in his lap, spilling what was left in it over his shabby tunic.

'Why? Does it matter?'

'Does it matter that one of the Templars' own knights, skilled at silent killing, was in Oxford when the Tartar commander was murdered? When hundreds of Templar knights and soldiers have been slaughtered in battle against the Tartars? I have probably been running down blind alleys all this time. I must go to Torold's Lane immediately.'

Abashed, Peter Bullock looked on as Falconer dashed out of the room.

Eleven

You will expect to come plundering, spoiling, and stripping
bare the ruins where men now live again, a people gathered
out of the nations, a people acquiring cattle and goods, and
making their home at the very centre of the world.

Ezekiel 38: 12–13

The unexpected coolness of the evening air – the first time
it had been so for days – halted Falconer's intemperate
rush down Great Bailey. And by the time he reached the High
Street, lit by the flaming torches of the tavern fronts, he had
reduced his progress to a stroll. There was, after all, no point
in confronting Guillaume de Beaujeu with an accusation of
murder. The Templar was both devious and imperturbable.
He could either deny the murder, whether he had committed
it or not, or even admit it, and defy Falconer's efforts to
prove it. No – by far the best course of action would be for
Falconer to do with de Beaujeu what he had requested Bullock
to do with Guchuluk. Merely observe, and hope for some
betrayal through either party's actions.

Resolved on a long, sleepless night, Falconer made a detour
to Aristotle's Hall to scavenge for some provisions that might
sustain him through the long hours to dawn. In the kitchen
he found a scrap of cold, fatty pork, and folded it inside a
hunk of dark, gritty manchet bread, thrusting the resulting
package into the purse at his waist. Striding back through
the hall, he was halted by a call from the gallery above. It
was Richard Youlden, the lad who had seen Yeh-Lu on his

foolish visit to the hall, and he seemed anxious to speak to his master.

'Yes, Richard, what is it? I am in a hurry.'

Richard looked abashed, but carried on: 'Thomas said you want to know of a good archer amongst the students. Well, there are several I know of – Philip Metcalf, Walter Colnet, John Stone and Benedict Tunstede are amongst the best.'

Falconer, intent on more important matters now, went to cut the youth off. But Richard was determined to speak his mind.

'But there is one who is as accurate with a longbow as all of those I have mentioned, and he has been talking recently of, as he put it, showing those Tartars a thing or two. I just thought you might like to know.'

Falconer realized that Richard Youlden had a mind sharper than his stolid, farm-boy appearance led everyone to believe. He had obviously put together Falconer's interest in archery, and the death of Chimbai, and provided a suspect. Falconer would not, however, confirm the lad's suspicions yet as to what he was pursuing. Still, he marvelled how one day he could be despairing of finding anyone with cause and opportunity to kill Chimbai, and the next day he had an embarrassment of riches. He might as well add this name to his growing list. 'And who is this paragon of the archer's skill?'

'Miles Bikerdyke.'

As night fell, and the stench of stale beer drifted up from the tavern below, Guillaume de Beaujeu prepared himself for the next act in his strategem. So far, with Chimbai's death, the plan that the Grand Master of the Templars had laid before him was unrolling perfectly. The old man had impressed upon him the need for absolute secrecy, and when he had heard what the master proposed, he was not surprised at this. At first, it had seemed like madness – the world turned upside down – but then the old man had unfolded the ancient parchment and revealed the truth that lay behind the events of the last thirty years. Although it had all begun much earlier than that – in the age of Alexander Magnus.

As the insects of the night chirruped on that cold Parisian evening, the Grand Master spoke hypnotically of Alexander the Great's letter to Aristotle, where he wrote of Sun and Moon trees that prophesied his own death. The master also made reference to a passage from *Iter ad Paradisum*, that mystical text of Alexander's travels, where Alexander went in search of an earthly Paradise. It described how he sailed up a great river so large it resembled a sea, and came to a mighty city. There he sent a knight in a boat to demand tribute from the citizens and their submission. An old man opened a high window in a wall overlooking the river, and for tribute dropped a small stone in the knight's boat.

'The meaning of the stone was explained to Alexander by a mystic,' said the Grand Master. 'He said it will outweigh any amount of gold, but sprinkle it with dust and it will be as light as a feather. So it was revealed by God that He favoured Alexander, but, like all men, he would come to a dusty death.'

De Beaujeu was puzzled, fearing that the old man was wandering, even losing his mind. 'And what has this to do with the Tartars?'

A knowing smile flickered across the Grand Master's lips. 'We therefore know from Alexander that there are more of God's wonders in the East.' He stretched out a hand for the creased and ancient document lying on the table between them. 'Now read this.'

De Beaujeu gently turned the dusty document round, and began to read the grey, indistinct letters. Soon his hands were trembling, and his heart fluttered in his chest.

By the power and virtue of God and the Lord Jesus Christ, King of Kings, know I am the greatest monarch under the Heavens. Seventy-two kings are under my rule, and my empire extends to the three Indias, including Farther India, where lies the body of Saint Thomas. In my dominions are the unclean nations whom Alexander Magnus walled up amongst the mountains of the North, and who will come forth in latter days. There are giant ants that dig for gold, the Fountain of Youth, pebbles that give out light, a Sea of Sand and Rivers of Stone. When I go to war I will be followed by ten thousand knights, and one hundred thousand foot. Twelve archbishops sit at my right hand, and twenty bishops at my left. I have now conceived a desire to visit the Holy Sepulchre, and fight the enemies of the Cross. Prepare for my coming.

'But this is . . .' De Beaujeu was not sure he dared say the name, so the Grand Master said it for him.

'Prester John.'

De Beaujeu felt a chill run up his spine that had nothing to do with the coldness of the room in which the two men sat.

Falconer was surprised that the normally circumspect de Beaujeu appeared distracted, almost careless, when he emerged from the cheap tavern in Torold's Lane. He had prepared himself for a long, dull, fruitless night hidden in the empty dwelling almost opposite the tavern. The ramshackle house, roofless and without any boards on the beams of the upper floor, was a fortuitous hiding place, and Falconer had settled down close to the narrow window looking out on to the lane. The shutters hung on broken hinges, but prevented the casual passer-by from seeing him. De Beaujeu was no casual observer, however, and Falconer was worried that following him unseen would be like trying to hide an elephant on the flat plain of Port Meadow.

Soon, his limbs felt stiff, and his back began to ache, but he dared not leave his post at the window for fear of missing de Beaujeu. The tavern was ill-frequented, with only the poorest forced to drink its badly brewed and often stale ale. So there was little happening in the lane to divert the bored and hungry Falconer. He watched a ragged individual enter, a hole in his breech-clout displaying his arse to the world. And then, after what seemed an eternity, he watched the same man leave, wiping his lips and spitting on the hard-packed earth of the lane as if trying to get the taste of the ale out of his mouth. There was no sound of revelry from inside the tavern – Falconer imagined the ale was not conducive to being cheerful. He was about to give in to hunger pangs and get the fatty pork parcel out of his purse when he saw another man emerge from the tavern. His clothes were patched and worn, but they hung from a well-built frame. As the man walked casually down the lane towards the teaching schools, Falconer could see he was a confident, self-assured individual entirely unlike anyone else he had seen in this quarter. His hair was long, dark and well-cut. It was de Beaujeu, and he was being unusually careless about blending in with his environment. Stuffing the soggy bread and pork back into his purse, Falconer eased some life into his aching limbs and followed the Templar.

The western end of Torold's Lane gave on to the street that ran along the inner edge of the north walls. A few yards to the left was Smith Gate, and it was here that de Beaujeu was heading. Falconer hung back at the end of Torold's Lane to see what the Templar was up to. The area round the gate was lit by the flames from the watchman's torch, and de Beaujeu strode confidently into the circle of light. He bent over the watchman where he sat at his post, but no conversation ensued. All Falconer heard was a soft jangle of keys, and then he saw de Beaujeu stepping over to the gate. In a moment he had inserted the heavy key, turned it and had left the city unobserved. Or so he assumed. Falconer hurried over to the watchman, expecting to find him dead. But when he got close enough for his weak eyes to see clearly, it was obvious the old fool was merely fast asleep, his misshapen bald head bobbing on his chest. Falconer tried the little wicket door set in the larger Smith Gate through which the Templar had gone, but it was locked. De Beaujeu had secured it from the outside.

Falconer had to think quickly. The way the Templar had approached the watchman suggested he knew the man would be asleep. If that was the case, it was likely he had used this means of sneaking out of the city before – possibly even on the night before Chimbai was killed. And if he still intended his activity to be a secret, he would return the same way before the old man ended his watch at dawn. Falconer could wait for him, but in the mean time, what was he doing? Was he carrying out another murder? Was Guchuluk to be his victim this time? He would check with Peter Bullock to see if the Tartar was still in his tent.

He hurried up the steps to the top of the walls where he hoped to find the constable. He was disappointed – the ramparts were devoid of life. He then thought that perhaps he would be able to spot de Beaujeu crossing the meadow, and call out a warning. He leaned out over the rough stone surface of the ramparts, pulling his eye-lenses out of his crumb-filled purse. The landscape was still blurred, and he cursed in frustration when he realized the glass was covered in fatty smears from his impromptu food parcel. Wiping the lenses on his sleeve, he decided the night was too dark anyway. Anything that moved on the meadow was invisible, and the Tartar tents were simply black cloth in a black field. He slumped into the embrasure with a sigh, then the breath was knocked from his body by an attack from behind. Someone was pressing him flat against the battlements, lifting his whole weight up, and putting him off balance. It was impossible for the Templar to have fooled him, and stayed inside the city, wasn't it? But he couldn't think who else his attacker might be. At any moment he felt he was going to be pitched over the wall, and, though he had worked hard at understanding the flight of birds, he had not mastered it yet. So he didn't relish the thought of an abrupt and hopeless experiment being forced on him now. The gruff voice of the constable came as a relief.

'Oh, it's you, William. I thought it was Gutch-a-look doubling back on me.'

Falconer felt his feet being lowered back to the ground, and he almost sank to the floor in his relief at not having to emulate Balthazar so soon. Then he realized what Bullock had said.

'Guchuluk? Has he been on the move, too?'

Bullock nodded. 'He sneaked out of the camp some time ago. But I saw him – got my night eyes, you see, from being up here since dusk. He was obviously up to no good, so I followed his progress from up here, until he went into the hovels around Beaumont, outside North Gate. I reckoned if I got down there quickily enough, I could track him. But by the time the watchman had let me out of the gate, he was gone. He might have seen me on the ramparts, of course, and deliberately gone out of his way to lose me. Or tried to stalk me. That's why I thought you were him.' He sighed. 'So I've got a wild Tartar, an anthrofo . . . what did you say that word for cannibal was?'

'Anthropophagus.' Falconer knew there was no point in protesting the Tartar's innocence of this particular accusation. Bullock was determined to label them all cannibals.

'I've got a . . . cannibal loose in the stews of Beaumont.'

Falconer smiled to himself. 'Perhaps he just wanted the services of one of the whores down there.'

Bullock snorted. 'Yes, and to eat her for dessert. Anyway, what are you doing up here? Aren't you supposed to be following our friendly Templar?'

Falconer remembered why he was on the ramparts in the first place. 'I was – he went out of Smith Gate. I'm afraid your watchman wasn't being very observant.'

'Walter was asleep again, I suppose.' Bullock clearly knew about the weakness of his watchman. 'He's useless, but he needs the money, poor old boy, and Smith Gate is as safe as houses, whether he is awake or not.'

Falconer reckoned the 'poor old boy' was a decade younger than Bullock himself, but refrained from pointing out the fact. 'At least if the Templar's target tonight was Guchuluk, then he wasn't in camp to be murdered. And, as it will be dawn soon, I imagine a frustrated de Beaujeu will be trying to sneak back into the city. I think I'll arrange to welcome him back.'

'And I'll join you. He has made a fool of my watchman, after all.'

Bellasez the Jew had hardly set foot outside the Domus Conversorum in two years. That the Black Friars had taken him in when his daughter died had been a great surprise to him. He had feared he would starve, with no one to support him in his old age, and then along came a Christian friar in his black robes, and offered him accommodation in a house on Fish Street. And a very comfortable house it was, too, where he was waited on not by some surly servant girl, but by the friar himself. In return, all the man asked was the pleasure of religious debate. The Dominican had expounded the Christian faith clearly and concisely. Bellasez had frequently tried to explain the Jewish faith to the friar, but he feared his mental powers were now waning. He could no longer sustain a convincing argument concerning his older and wiser faith, and now had resorted to the strategy of at least not disagreeing with the friar. It seemed to please him, and that pleased Bellasez, as he didn't want to offend his host and benefactor.

Now he was glad he could help the friar in a more positive way. The man had come to the house in a sorry state some days ago. He couldn't remember exactly when – one day was very much like another, and time seemed to fly by of late. It must have been a number of days, for he had arrived at the house bleeding and sore, and now his wounds were scabbed and healing. He had tried to conceal a weapon under his cloak, but had fainted away; Bellasez had removed the nasty thing, and put it somewhere safe. It was typical of his memory that he couldn't quite remember where that was at the moment. Not that it mattered, for neither he nor the friar had need of it.

As he shuffled along the streets, stirring with life in the early morning light, he half-closed his eyes and recited his instructions again. If he repeated them regularly enough, he was sure he would not forget what he was meant to do. The last time he had gone on an errand for his daughter – of blessed memory – he had got no farther than Carfax, only to find himself in the centre of the crossroads with not an idea why he was there. He had had to return to incur the sharpness of Saphira's tongue. This errand was too important for that to happen again. He was going to meet his brethren – members of the Ten Lost Tribes of Israel, who had abandoned the Law of Moses and worshipped the Golden Calf, and whom God had enclosed beyond the Caspian Mountains – who now had once again come forth into the world.

The Christian traders setting up their stalls looked with amusement at the pale, spectre of a Jew shuffling along North

Gate Street. His head was no more than a skull stretched with grey parchment skin, devoid of hair. His robe was patched and stained, and he had nothing on his feet but woollen buskins. He was walking along mumbling some Jewish hocus-pocus to himself, over and over again. Clearly he was mad, and they soon ignored him and returned to their work.

Bellasez, oblivious to their derision, continued reciting his litany as he progressed: 'Go to the Tartars. Find the priest David. Bring him back to the Domus. Go to the Tartars. Find the priest . . . David, yes, David. Bring him back. And what was the other bit? Oh, yes – tell him I have a confession to make.'

Falconer and Bullock decided not to wait for de Beaujeu at Smith Gate. Oxford was beginning to rouse, and there would soon be people on the streets. They would be busy, but everyone had time to poke their noses into other people's business, and a confrontation at the gate would have quickly gathered an audience. What they had to say to the Templar required privacy, and the two men decided to accost him in his lodgings.

They reached the inn just as the first rays of sun poked exploratory fingers down the dusty lengths of Torold's Lane. The greyish hovels that lined the lane rejected the warmth, and only appeared dirtier and more ramshackle in the sun's pale light. If de Beaujeu had intended to remain unrecognized in Oxford, he should have stayed in this quarter. No one who knew his face would have walked through these shabby alleys. But he had made the mistake of carrying out his clandestine activity just where Peter Bullock had chosen to carry out his sentry duty. An unfortunate coincidence that had led to his exposure.

Falconer was all for waiting in the empty house across the lane from the inn that he had used as a hiding place in the night. But Bullock scorned this cautious approach, and went straight into the inn. The look of fear on the innkeeper's face at the sight of the constable on his premises soon assured the two men of access to the Templar's room – and a closed mouth from the innkeeper when de Beaujeu returned. He would be too fearful of the constable discovering his watered barrels of stale beer, if he did anything other than what Bullock demanded.

The Templar was not long in coming, for hardly had Bullock settled down on the creaking bed that was the room's sole item of furniture than Falconer heard footsteps on the stairs. They came towards the door of the room, then there was silence. As the moments passed, the two men exchanged puzzled glances. Had it been de Beaujeu, after all, or another lodger? But there were no other rooms on this upper floor – this one being squeezed into the space between the beams that formed the sharply angled eaves of the building. Bullock could contain himself no longer, and, despite Falconer's hissed protest, went over to the door and pulled it open.

'Ahh. Master Bullock, as I live and breathe.'

Falconer recognized the amused tones of Guillaume de Beaujeu immediately. He had known there was someone in the room, and had merely tried their patience with a waiting game. Bullock turned away from the door in disgust, and the Templar followed him in, sheathing a dagger in the scabbard hidden beneath his peasant's rough woollen cloak.

'And Regent Master William Falconer, too. I am honoured by your attendance. The setting could be more salubrious, but you know my order insists on poverty and humility.'

There was nothing humble about this man, in Falconer's estimation. He had realized his presence was uncovered, and yet was still in perfect control of the situation. It had been foolish to imagine they could catch him off his guard. He stood easily in the doorway, his feet set apart to brace himself, should the two men be mad enough to attack him. His face, smudged with dirt to conceal him in ·the night, was calm, but his eyes, brown pools with deep, dark centres, were alert. His thick, dark hair hung to his broad shoulders, and everything about his features belied the tattered clothes he was now dressed in. With no need for subterfuge, he had once again assumed the confident stance of Guillaume de Beaujeu, Knight Commander of the Templars.

Bullock was wearied by this posturing – it was for young men, who had time on their hands. He eased his aching back against the crumbling wall of the room and sighed, listening to the scurrying sound of rats above their heads in the rafters.

'Just tell him we know everything, William.'

De Beaujeu cocked his head in apparent amusement.

'Everything? What is this everything that you know?'

Falconer, too, felt tired of playing games, and was all for revealing what he knew – or thought he knew. But something he saw in the Templar's eyes stopped him. He reckoned he could discern a distant glint of some high purpose, a goal beyond mortal comprehension. And it was a spark he had not seen in the man's eyes before – de Beaujeu had seemed such a down-to-earth man, almost in spite of his spiritual vows. Now, he seemed to have found a purpose beyond simply battling for the Holy Land, and it scared Falconer a little. He decided to prevaricate some more.

'We know that you have been in Oxford some days, and that you are here in disguise for some reason.'

De Beaujeu snorted in derision, holding his arms wide to display his peasant's rags. 'It does not take a regent master of Oxford University to work that one out. What else do you know?'

'Tell him, William.' Bullock was getting impatient.

'We have observed you sneaking out of Smithy Gate in the middle of the night. And it does not take a regent master – 'it was Falconer's turn to be sarcastic – '. . . to put your presence and your movements together with the arrival of the Tartar embassy which is accessible from both North and Smith Gates.' He paused only for a moment, then plunged on. 'Nor with the death of the ambassador, Noyan Chimbai.'

Falconer was not really expecting any response from the Templar, imagining he would face the accusation with impassive features. So he was surprised when de Beaujeu's calm features split into a broad grin, and was shocked when the man burst into uproarious laughter. Falconer and Bullock looked at each other in puzzlement, while the Templar struggled to regain his composure.

'Would you care to explain your hilarity at the accusation?' Bullock was not as thick-skinned as Falconer, and flushed at being found so amusing. 'You steal a key from my watchman . . .'

'Who is so watchful he hardly stirs when I take it from his belt.' De Beaujeu's grin reappeared, threatening to break out into laughter again.

Bullock pressed on: 'You take a key, break the city curfew, and commit murder in the environs of the city for which I am responsible.'

'And can you prove this accusation of murder?' De Beaujeu was restored to his normal equanimity, though the creases as the corner of his eyes still betrayed his amusement. 'Though I plead guilty to the other charges – and you should be grateful to me for exposing a weakness in your impregnable defences – I cannot see how you could find cause to say I killed the Tartar.'

Bullock, stubborn as ever, was losing his temper. 'You are a renowned assassin, and you were wandering the night before it happened. And you were out there tonight again to continue your little crusade. That is enough for me.'

De Beaujeu winced at the word assassin, coined for the Eastern, drug-crazed murderers who killed at the instigation of the Old Man of the Mountain. It struck too close to the image he feared the Grand Master and fellow Templars had of him to be lightly tossed off.

'You may care to know that it was a Tartar army that destroyed the Order of Assassins in their stronghold at Mulchet. So we have them to thank for that at least.' He placed his hands against the rotten timber that crossed the room just above his head and leaned forwards, filling the room with his presence. 'And we may have cause to thank them for a good deal more in the future.'

Bullock could see he was getting nowhere, and looked pleadingly at Falconer. Seeing his friend either could not, or would not, give him any further support, he stormed out of the room, brushing the younger man aside with the back of his hand. Falconer, too, made to leave, but, as he passed the Templar, de Beaujeu took his arm and whispered in his ear:

'The Templars are not seeking the downfall of the Tartars – quite the opposite. I will say no more. But if you want to know of a man who hates them enough to kill, then you should talk to Sir Hugh Leyghton about his Templar brother, Geoffrey.'

Twelve

I will pour down teeming rain, hailstones hard as rock, and fire and brimstone, upon him, upon his squadrons, upon the whole concourse of peoples with him. Thus will I prove myself great and holy and make myself known to many nations.

Ezekiel 38:22

He knew it was going to be a dreadful day when he saw the stone fall from the roof of the Church of St Mary and nearly strike Count Henry on the head. The ill omen was ignored by those who witnessed it, but its import would not go away. If he closed his eyes, he could see the four divisions of Henry's army drawn up on the plain beyond Leignitz. And in the centre were the Silesian and Moravian armies along with the Hospitallers and Templars. Standing out in their midst was Geoffrey, tall and handsome, his head unhelmed, with the sun striking off his golden hair. He wanted to cry out a warning, but no sound would come from his throat. And even if he had managed to call out, the jangling noise of the horse armour, and the chaotic cries of the army's commanders, would have drowned him out. He begged Geoffrey just to look back – to see him one last time – but their eyes didn't meet. Geoffrey only had eyes for the enemy, which was now ranged on the farthest edge of the plain. They were massed like a sea of ants – a hundred of them for every man in the Christian army – and a single, mournful sigh escaped the lips of the assembled knights at the sight. The Tartar vanguard advanced in close order, and Henry, on seeing their numbers were so small, sent in his own horsemen together with the Teutonic Knights. The Tartars began to retreat, and, to press home his advantage, Henry committed the Templars and Hospitallers to the fray. Waving his sword in the air, the bare-headed Geoffrey led the charge towards the fleeing Tartars. His hair streamed out behind him, and the black and white Templar banner fluttered above him. Then he was in the midst of battle, swinging his sword to left and right and carving a swathe through the little horsemen. Bernard gloried in his manliness, until a swirling mist suddenly enveloped the Christian army. It built into a thick cloud of noxious yellow fumes, and Geoffrey was gone from sight.

Bernard called out in his sleep, but the nightmare was destined to continue to its inexorable end. The flight of the Tartar army had been a trap, and the Templar and Hospitaller knights, blundering around in the smoke, were cut down by a hail of arrows. When it cleared, all Bernard could see were bodies, a mountain of corpses, covered in blood. At the top of the horrendous mound lay Geoffrey, his breast pierced by a dozen arrows. His face swam into view, contorted and fearful, with gouts of dark blood pouring from the corners of his eyes like tears. As Bernard looked on in horror, the flesh fell from Geoffrey's face, leaving a bleached and eyeless skull. All around was the stink of rotting bodies – the stench filled the sleeping man's nostrils. He tossed and turned, his face screwed up in revulsion. Then he was alone with Geoffrey, cradling him in his arms. He looked down into the horror of his face, and his bony jaw opened, creaking like an un-oiled door. Geoffrey began to speak.

Bernard awoke with a start, sweating, knowing he would never hear Geoffrey's last words. The nightmare always ended at this point in the awful saga. He rolled from the narrow cot on which he lay and pulled his rumpled, stinking robe into some semblance of order. He had not washed or changed his linen since seeking refuge in the Domus Conversorum, and every night the visions came, haunting him and drenching him in sweat. He knew his one companion, Bellasez, did not care about the smell – he rarely washed himself. The malodorous nature of the Jew-convert had irritated the normally fastidious Bernard in the past. Now, he did not notice the smell of his companion, nor could he care less about the state of his own body. And where the ramblings of the old man had annoyed him beyond comprehension as he strove for his soul, he now quite enjoyed his undemanding company. At least Bellasez did not ask how he had come to be in the state he was, and why he did not leave the house.

He had spent a few blessed days imagining he could ignore the world and what he had done, blanking his mind to the consequences. But in the early hours of this morning, he had fancied he could hear the matins bell ringing at Trill Mill, and knew he must set matters right. Rousing the bewildered Bellasez from his bed, he had sat with him in the dark, tutoring the old man in what he had to do and say as soon as it got light. Bellasez had nodded, splashing spittle down the front of Bernard's black robe. The friar had not been sure if the Jew-convert really understood, but he was Bernard's only hope. He sent Bellasez on his way, and closed the door behind him quickly, so as not to be noticed by the tradesmen, who were already beginning to stir on what was another ordinary day for them. A day of reckoning for Bernard. Exhausted, he had returned to his cot, and fallen straight back to sleep. It had been then that the nightmare had returned.

Making his way across the marshy ground towards the Dominican friary, Falconer wondered what the import of Guillaume de Beaujeu's words might be. He had suggested

Falconer speak to Sir Hugh Leyghton about his brother Geoffrey, who was a Templar. Did he mean that Geoffrey was likely to have killed Chimbai? But for what reason? If Sir Hugh held the key to the puzzle, then he would get the truth out of him one way or another. The king's ambassador was staying at the Dominican friary, where one of their number was acting as his secretary. With the puzzle niggling at his brain, Falconer resolved to follow this loose thread, even though the weave of clues was beginning to unravel in many directions at once. He hoped that this might be the one clue to provide him with a framework to hold everything together.

At first the friary appeared as calm and peaceful as it always did, with the Black Friars going about their business in their usual purposeful way. But when he asked a friar in the herb garden if Sir Hugh Leyghton was still lodged in the guest house, he detected an undercurrent of unease. The friar remained bent over his weeding, and mumbled some words that were lost in the hood that slipped over his shoulders as he kept to his task. Falconer frowned at this unusual discourtesy, but continued on his way. Crossing the courtyard in front of the guest quarters, he was aware of eyes following him, and he turned round in time to see the back of a friar scurrying into the day chapel. He wondered what Sir Hugh might have done to warrant such odd behaviour. Maybe he would soon find out.

He stepped from the bright sunshine into the unlit lower hall of the guest quarters, so it was a few moments before he saw Sir Hugh and Brother Adam Grasse standing in a huddle over the fireplace. It was not for the sake of warmth, for the day was hot, and cold ashes lay in the hearth. Both men were looking over their shoulders guiltily, as if caught in some sort of conspiracy. Falconer stood in the doorway, uncertain of his ground. It was the friar who first recognized Falconer, and strode over, followed by Sir Hugh, who was clearly having some difficulty remembering where he had seen the master before. Then comprehension dawned, and he recalled the self-assured scholar whom he had mistaken for the chancellor the night of the Tartar banquet. His natural joviality somewhat fabricated today, Grasse pressed Falconer's right hand in both his warm, slippery palms, and asked him what he could do for him.

Falconer smiled. 'In fact, it is Sir Hugh that I am seeking.'

Leyghton's eyebrows shot up in curiosity, and he exchanged a glance with Brother Adam. The portly friar took the hint, and left the two men together. Leyghton looped his thumbs through the heavy belt at his waist, and assumed a casual air that sat ill with his earlier guilty expression.

'What is it you want of me, Master . . . er . . . Falconer. I am a busy man, with the king's business to attend to. The death of the Tartar has not put an end to the negotiations I must undertake.'

'Indeed, it is the noyan's death that I am here to enquire about. And the whereabouts of your brother.'

Leyghton paled and rocked back on his heels. A hiss of breath escaped his lips, then he recovered himself. His reply was not at all what Falconer had expected.

'My elder brother, Geoffrey – and I have no other brother, so it must be he you are asking about – has been dead these twenty-seven years past. So if you think he killed the Tartar, you could not be more in error. Though if he lived, he would have good reason to kill, for many of his comrades died alongside him as a result of a cowardly manœuvre by the Tartar army at Leignitz.'

Falconer knew of the slaughter at Leignitz, of course. He had been a young man at the time, and the destruction of the flower of Christian chivalry by these mysterious monsters from the East had reverberated around the world. So Geoffrey Leyghton had died there. Then what had de Beaujeu meant by his comment – or had Falconer misconstrued it? Had he meant the brother – the man standing before Falconer – could be the murderer? But Sir Hugh had been in Shrewsbury meeting the king at the time, hadn't he? Trying to recover from this further blow to his investigation, he said the first thing that came into his head.

'He was a Templar?'

'Yes, and I was proud of him, and modelled my life on him, though I have not taken the Templar vows. I am my parents' only child now, and must continue the family line. Celibacy is not an option for me.'

'And all his comrades died with him, you say?'

Leyghton nodded grimly. 'Except for one, whose leg had been broken falling from his horse the day before the battle. He lived, but with considerably more broken than his leg after that day. He left the order, but didn't abandon his faith, and became a Dominican friar.'

'Do you know where he now lives?'

'Of course. You saw him with me in the Tartar's tent. His name is Brother Bernard – Bernard de Genova.'

Falcolner saw the slenderest of threads being offered him.

'And might I speak with Brother Bernard?'

Leyghton smiled grimly. 'That is impossible. You see, what I was discussing with Brother Adam when you arrived was the apparent disappearance of Bernard. He had not been seen for days.'

Falconer's face clouded over, and he stared intently at the knight, wondering if Brother Bernard was really missing, or if he, Falconer, was being deliberately kept from pursuing his goal. Leyghton guessed what was in his mind.

'Let Brother Adam show you Bernard's cell, if you like.

And ask the rest of the Black Friars. After all, not everyone can be in this conspiracy of silence you so obviously suspect me of.'

Falconer curtly nodded his head, and went in search of Adam Grasse. The fat man seemed happy to show Falconer Bernard's cell. But to Falconer's disappointment, there was nothing there to assist his investigation. The cell was stark and cool, with nothing to distinguish it from any other friar's cell. Falconer took in the large crucifix hung on the lime-washed walls directly over the head of the narrow bed, and the simple lectern that stood in one corner. There was no candle nor even runnels of molten wax at the lectern to suggest anyone had stood there recently. He crossed over to the bed, and lifted the woollen blanket that covered the thin mattress, feeling the surface of the ticking with his hand. Everything was pristine, clean and cold. Either Bernard de Genova was inordinately tidy, or his room had been cleaned of anything that might suggest his involvement with the murder of Noyan Chimbai.

When Falconer looked up at Adam Grasse, his hand still resting on the mattress, he saw a shifty look in the friar's eyes. Then, though the friar held his gaze, a ruddy flush started on his neck and crept inexorably over his pallid cheeks. Falconer was not going to let him escape.

'Has this cell been cleaned since Bernard disappeared?'

Grasse's reddening cheeks quivered. 'I am not sure what you are implying.'

Noticing that the friar had evaded his question, Falconer nevertheless continued. The evasion was sufficient confirmation of his suspicions.

'Is there something about Brother Bernard's past that it was necessary to hide?'

'I . . . I'm not sure I know what you mean. Bernard was a

Templar before he joined the Order of St Dominic, and I am sure he led a blameless life before he came here.'

By now Grasse's face was a uniform red, and he clearly wished he were not in Falconer's presence. The regent master pressed home his advantage.

'And recently? In conducting his daily business in and around the friary. Or in his capacity as Sir Hugh's secretary.'

The friar coughed nervously, prepared to offer Falconer something at least to explain his embarrassment. 'He . . . er . . . did seem sorely troubled at the time of the first meeting with the Tartars. And . . .'

Grasse hesitated, and Falconer urged him on: 'And what?'

Somehow, though Grasse had wanted to keep this quiet, the sharp-eyed scholar seemed to draw confidences out of him. 'He was seen returning to the friary by the night gate the morning the body was discovered in the Tartar camp. One of the lay brothers, going to ring the matins bell, says he saw Brother Bernard enter his cell, and close the door.'

'What sort of state was he in?'

'State? The lay brother did not say, other than that he was worried about the brother because . . .' The friar was still reluctant, but finally he said what was on his mind: '. . . because he thought he saw blood on Bernard's face.'

'And where did you think he had been?'

'Been?' The normally self-assured Grasse now realized he had been sucked into telling more than he had intended. Now he was reduced to repeating Falconer's questions while desperately trying to plan his response.

'You must have been concerned that a brother was breaking the rules of the order, and sneaking around at night.'

Grasse suddenly found himself on easier ground, huffing and puffing self-righteously at the suggestion his order lived merely by rules. 'We are not like some of the older monastic orders, whose life has become a sterile repetition. We Dominicans are here for a purpose. And Brother Bernard, most of all, concerned himself with teaching and practical work. Why, he gladly took over the running of the Jewish Converts' House recently, and immersed himself in the work of conversion.'

He suddenly stopped, and gasped. Falconer finished the friar's thought for him:

'And no one tried the Converts' House when Bernard disappeared?'

Grasse dropped his eyes. 'I'm afraid not.'

'Then I will go and look for you.' Falconer imagined he heard a noise outside in the cloister, but by the time he had crossed the little room and lifted the stiff and cumbersome latch on the door, he could see no one in the vicinity of Bernard's cell. Maybe it had been imagination, but he wondered where Sir Hugh was now. As he set off to find Bernard, the fat Breton called after him:

'I shall pray that you find Brother Bernard safe and well.'

The recipient of Adam Grasse's prayers was at that moment himself praying for forgiveness. Before him stood the somewhat disconcerted Kerait Mongol and Nestorian Christian, David. He had been abruptly roused from his far-from-peaceful slumbers by Sigatay. Opening his bleary eyes, he saw that the churlish soldier had an unaccustomed grin spread across his pock-marked face.

'You have a visitor.'

Thinking he was the butt of some soldier's joke, David had protested at being woken up, and pulled the animal skin back over his head. Sigatay cursed him roundly, and kicked him in the small of the back.

'I think he wants to see you now. Or shall I tell the bahadur that he's here?'

The last thing David wanted was for Guchuluk to be dragged out of his bed to find his interpreter receiving a visitor from the English. He had felt the bahadur's eyes on him for the last couple of days, and was trying hard to remain inconspicuous. Better to be the butt of Sigatay's joke than incur Guchuluk's anger and suspicion. Grumbling at being disturbed, in order to cover his fear, David rose and poked his head out of the yurt's door flap. What he saw resembled a skeleton that had been decked in pauper's clothes and animated by strings. The old man, if he truly were a living creature, hopped from one bootless foot to the other, and muttered continually under his breath. Spotting the priest, and the cross that hung round his neck, he suddenly shot forward and rattled off an incantation. Making a fearful sign of the cross to ward off evil spirits, David shrank back towards the safety of the yurt, still not sure if a game was being played with him. The demon repeated his incantation, this time more slowly, and David recognized some of the words.

In the midst of other expostulations, Bellasez managed, 'Find the priest David . . . I have a confession. May the Lord help me, I can remember no more.'

Even then, David might have dismissed the apparition as a madman – who in this land would want to confess to a foreign priest, holding beliefs heretical to the Church of Rome? But the old man grabbed his wrist with a claw that was unexpectedly strong, and pulled him out of the yurt. So, not without trepidation, David had allowed himself to be brought to Bernard de Genova. The only difficult moment was when his captor dragged him past the scrutiny of the stallholders inside the city walls, but they ignored his sallow skin and the Eastern cast to his face, assuming, as he was in the company of Bellasez, that he was another mad Jew.

Now he was beginning to wonder who was truly mad –

himself, the ancient who dragged him here, or the religious who knelt before him. The friar was clad all in black, which made his pasty face all the more ghastly. The wild look in his eyes spoke of torment the like of which the Nestorian could not conceive. And he babbled incessantly, mingling personal tales with passages from the Bible and mad interpretations that David little understood. He could do no more than place a consoling hand on the friar's head, while the old man who had brought him to this madhouse looked benignly on. Meanwhile Bernard de Genova developed his thesis.

'Like everyone in the West, I saw your people as monstrous and inhuman, and something to be expunged. But are we not taught that God created every race of men of one stock, to inhabit the whole earth's surface? But still I could see no farther than the pain of the lost souls around me. I cursed your kind, and I have plotted death. But the other night, I was visited with a vision. If you truly are a plague on mankind, as was written, then you are but the tool of a vengeful God sent against a sinful world. Is it not written in Revelation – "God said, Release the four angels held bound at the River Euphrates. So the four angels were let loose to kill a third of mankind. And their squadron of cavalry, whose count I heard, numbered two hundred million."'

Bernard clutched hard at David's quilted jacket, and drew in a great breath that racked his body to its core.

'If you truly are the hammer of God, then you should strike me, for I have sinned against God, and deserve to be punished. And I know the cause of your leader's death.'

David paled, not daring to believe what the friar had just said, but afraid to ask him to repeat it. This was dangerous knowledge indeed. He began to rack his brain as to how he was going to cope with this, while Bernard continued reciting Revelation, lost in the smoke of the battle of Leignitz:

'"And the horses had heads like lions' heads, and out of their mouths came fire, smoke, and sulphur. By these three plagues, that is, by the fire, the smoke, and the sulphur that came from their mouths, a third of mankind was killed."'

The Bahadur Guchuluk was feeling peculiarly exposed. Having decided to keep an eye on the priest, he had been put in a dilemma when the madman had dragged David away from the Tartar camp towards the city. But it had not taken him long to come to the conclusion that this might be the only opportunity he had to find out what the man was doing. Perhaps he had formed an alliance with his co-religionists, and was now going to meet them. Guchuluk flung a hooded cloak over his distinctive quilted jackets and woollen trousers, and crossed the open meadow at an angle to the route David and his guide were taking. Keeping them in sight, he made his way directly towards the hovels that lined the approach to the North Gate. Having passed down a narrow alley and on to the main thoroughfare, he joined the steady stream of travellers that was beginning to fill the dusty road.

He lost sight of his quarry momentarily as they entered the gate, and he hesitated in case he was uncovered. But to his disgust at the lack of security, he walked unchallenged through the now bustling gateway. As it was early morning, the street was not as full as it would be a few hours later, and he glanced around to find the two men. He saw them instantly, for the old madman was waving his arms in the air, and barking some incantation to the heavens. This would be an easy pursuit. He followed them through the market and across an intersection of highways at the centre of the city. He couldn't help noting in his mind details that might stand him in good stead should they ever need to mount an attack on the city. It was while his gaze was thus diverted that they disappeared. He almost panicked, remembering that he could not ask anyone where they might have gone. Then he spotted an open door in a narrow, drab-looking building squashed between the stalls of two fishmongers. Even as he peered into the gloom behind the door, it closed on him. He had to assume that was where his quarry had gone to ground. Looking around, he saw across the street a large building with a tower. And at the base of the tower was a bolted door set in a deep recess. There he settled himself in the shadows of the stone arch, hoping he looked like a beggar availing himself of a cosy nook to rest. The strategy obviously worked, for none of the market traders or their early-morning customers gave him a second look. Now all he had to do was to be patient, and await his opportunity.

Sir Hugh Leyghton was shocked by the import of what he heard Bernard confess. At first he could not believe it – didn't want to believe it – but somehow he knew it was true. For the second time today, he had been forced to eavesdrop at closed doors in order to discover what he needed to know. The first time, he had followed the meddling scholar Falconer and Adam Grasse back to Bernard's cell. He did not trust the friar, and needed to ensure Grasse kept his part of their bargain of secrecy about the missing man. At least Grasse had removed the bloodstained mattress in time, and replaced it with a clean one. Leyghton had convinced him that, by this means, he was ensuring that no suspicion would fall on the order concerning the death of the Tartar. And of course Leyghton knew the stratagem would also keep his embassy out of the mire of suspicion – until de Genova should be found. He only had to be sure he found him first.

Grasse had at first handled the Oxford scholar well, and Leyghton had been going to leave his post at the door when he was alarmed to hear Grasse weaken under the hectoring of the scholar, and almost admit Bernard's guilt. He had been on the point of bursting in on the interrogation when he, too, grasped the import of Grasse mentioning the House of Converts. Stopping only to ask a friar the location of the Domus, he had hurried through the thronging streets to keep ahead of Falconer. Without a plan in his head, he had been about to enter the Domus when he heard Bernard's voice coming from the other side of the door. He was talking with someone, and Sir Hugh did not want anyone else to know he was here. Once again he had stationed himself outside a closed door and eavesdropped – on Bernard's long and rambling confession.

Passing over Grandpont on his return from the Dominican friary, Falconer was surprised to find Roger Bacon seated on the low parapet, dangling his legs over the stream below. His grey Franciscan robe was pulled up to his thighs and his bare toes dripped water. The great 'Doctor Admirabilis' had been paddling. Concerned that the man had at last lost his mind, Falconer tapped him gently on the shoulder. He was rewarded with a broad smile, and a cry of recognition.

'William! Am I glad you are here – I have been meaning to talk to you. Have you been avoiding me?'

'Me avoiding you? I have called on you, but you seemed more than a little preoccupied every time.'

Bacon grunted. 'Maybe I have. But I was working on something requiring precision. And then I lost part of it, and had to go to the smith to get him to replace it. And the fool just didn't appreciate how accurate his work had to be. Still, you do not want to know my worries – it looks as though you have plenty of your own.'

He swung his legs off the parapet and pushed his toes into the discarded sandals that lay at the roadside. 'Tell me what is on your mind, and perhaps I can help.'

Falconer, conscious that he wanted to get to the Domus Conversorum as soon as possible, decided it was still worth enlisting Bacon's help in assembling the few clues he had to Chimbai's murder. As they walked through the South Gate, he explained how the murder had taken place at around the time Bacon, Yeh-Lu and he were talking in Roger's tower. But that it had happened in a guarded tent, possibly by a very accurate or very lucky archer.

'Many had reason to kill him, but none the opportunity, it seems,' commented Falconer glumly. 'I have discovered that the chancellor, de Ewelme, had employed a student on some secret mission. His name is Miles Bikerdyke, and he is reckoned a good archer. So that is a possibility. And anyone in the Tartar camp may have done it, but I have had little chance to uncover any motives because no one will talk to me.'

Bacon smiled. 'I may be able to help you there. I travelled across the Channel with Chimbai and his entourage. And what I saw suggested there was no love lost between him and his young assistant.'

'Guchuluk?'

'That's the one. But tell me, why are we searching for a missing Dominican in connection with this murder?'

Falconer took a deep breath, and explained how he had suspected a Templar by the name of Guillaume de Beaujeu of the murder. But when he had confronted the man, de Beaujeu had convinced him of his innocence. He in turn, however, advised Falconer to check on another Templar. Or rather the younger brother of a Templar long dead. Therefore, by the most circuitous route, he was led to Sir Hugh Leyghton, the very man now in Oxford treating with the Tartars for the king, even though his Templar brother had been killed by Tartars. Moreover, Hugh Leyghton's secretary, Bernard de Genova, had been a fellow Templar of Leyghton's brother, only avoiding death at the hands of the Tartars twenty-seven years earlier by virtue of a riding accident. Though the connections were convoluted, and the whole story stretched the imagination, Bacon agreed there was more than sheer coincidence at play here.

'And this same Bernard de Genova is the Dominican supposedly holed up in the Domus Conversorum?'

Falconer nodded. 'And he was seen covered in blood on the day of the murder.'

'Then your syllogism goes as follows: All murderers are bloodied; Bernard was bloodied; therefore Bernard is a murderer?'

Like some raw student, Falconer was drawn into nodding eager agreement. Bacon then triumphantly revealed the holes in the false argument.

'Except my landlord, the skinner, is frequently bloodied due to his trade. And he is not a murderer – of men, anyway. And you said that the Tartar was killed with an arrow. Unless it was fired from within the tent, and at close quarters, the murderer would have escaped untainted. So your whole syllogism is fallacious.'

Falconer knew Bacon was right – the same thoughts had been in his head all along. But he had been reluctant to give them credence. There was, after all, something strange about Bernard's behaviour that demanded he find the man, and at least discover why he had been covered in blood, and why he was so scared.

Still the portentous words echoed in Bernard's skull.

Then I saw an angel coming down from heaven with the key of the abyss and a great chain in his hands. He seized the dragon, that serpent of old, the Devil or Satan, and chained him up for a thousand years; he threw him into the abyss, shutting and sealing it over him, so that he might seduce the nations no more till the thousand years were over . . . Then Satan will be let loose from his dungeon; and he will come out to seduce the nations in the four quarters of the earth.

He knew he had done wrong and deserved his punishment, so long delayed. So when he heard the footsteps and raised his head, he was not surprised by whom he saw. Satan had come to take his own, and he called out the name in his heart.

'Geoffrey.'

Thirteen

I will bring you against my land, that the nations may know me, when they see me prove my holiness at your expense, O Gog.

Ezekiel 38: 16

When he later tried to put the confusion of events into their proper order, Falconer found it very difficult – even though he and Roger had witnessed the outcome themselves. What they had seen as they pushed through the mêlée that was the Fish Street market was an ashen Sir Hugh Leyghton emerging from the doorway of the Domus Conversorum. There was blood on his hands, and he left a long smear of it down the doorpost as he stumbled and clutched it to support himself. He took a deep breath, then, looking up, saw the two scholars staring at him in consternation. He moved his lips, but nothing more than a croak emerged. Taking another great gulp of air, he lurched towards Falconer and Bacon, and managed to speak:

'He is dead – he has been murdered.'

Afterwards, Bacon insisted that Leyghton took some moments to make his statement. Falconer thought he called out immediately, as though he was intent on starting the hue and cry the moment he came out of the door. Whatever the truth of it, both men rushed over to Leyghton, who looked as though he were about to collapse.

Falconer spoke first: 'Who is dead?'

Leyghton's face was bloodless, and his breathing shallow. He seemed unable to speak.

'Is it Bernard?'

Sir Hugh managed a gloomy nod of the head. Falconer and Bacon both cautiously entered the doorway set part-way into the grimy alley that ran through to the back yard of the house. They found themselves in the shabby hall of the Converts' House. Inside, it was difficult to see, as the shutters on to the street were closed, and only a narrow window high on the farthest wall shed light into the room. But as their eyes adjusted, the enormity of the deed became clear. The body of Bernard de Genova was indeed a sorry sight.

He was lying crumpled up on his right side, his knees tucked underneath him, and his arms extended. It was as though he had been kneeling in prayer when he was killed. It was obvious how he had died, for his neck had been slashed, and the wound gaped horribly, like an obscene mouth. There was blood all over his black Dominican habit, and a great gout of blood was splashed across the packed clay floor. The pressure of blood in the body had caused it to be expelled with great force – there were even splash marks and runnels on the far wall. Falconer guessed that unless the killer had stood behind him to cut his throat, he would be covered in Bernard's blood. And, even if he had, his hands would be bloody. The left side of Bernard's head was also a mess of matted hair and blood. The smell of death was overpowering, and both men compressed their lips, swallowing hard. Bacon was all for leaving, but Falconer knew he had to examine the body more closely, if he was not to lose more clues, as he had done with the disastrous burning of the Tartar tent. He bent over the body, his eye-lenses to his face, curious about the apparent second wound to the side of Bernard's face. As he was examining the body more closely and taking note of the old, healed cuts on Bernard's arms, Roger peered at something on the floor, poking it with the toe of his sandal. It was a pinkish lump, lying close to the edge of the lake of blood. He grunted in disgust, and Falconer looked round to see the find. He tentatively picked it up between the forefinger and thumb, and looked more closely. It was one of Bernard's ears, and it was still warm to the touch.

In the doorway, Sir Hugh groaned. 'It's him – the Tartar. The monster's mutilated him, just as his fellow creatures did at Leignitz.'

Leyghton's whole frame was twitching, as though he were standing barefoot on hot coals. Falconer realized he would have to be kept occupied, or he would go blundering into the Tartar camp demanding Guchuluk's surrender. He might even try to slaughter him before the eyes of his fellow soldiers, and the consequences of that could be unimaginable for the town and university. He quickly asked Leyghton to alert the authorities in the shape of the town constable.

'We need him here as soon as possible, Sir Hugh, so that we are seen to act swiftly but within the law.'

Leyghton hesitated for but a moment, holding his blood-stained hands in the air as if in mute accusation. Then he nodded curtly, and left the two men alone, agitatedly wiping his hands down the sides of his embroidered surcoat. Bacon waited until he had gone, then he looked thoughtfully at Falconer.

'Could it have been Guchuluk? Did you see him out there, too?'

Falconer knew what Bacon meant. Before Sir Hugh had come staggering out of the Domus, he had been sure he had spotted the Tartar weaving his way through the press of people in the market. At first all he saw was someone oddly clad for the hot and sticky day – the cloaked and hooded shape of a stocky man hurrying north towards Carfax. But as the figure pushed through the crowd, he looked back fleetingly, and

Falconer was sure he recognized the sallow features of Guchuluk under the hood. Before he could say anything to Bacon, Sir Hugh had appeared, and the moment had passed. And perhaps he was just remembering how Yeh-Lu had disguised himself, and imagining something more sinister about what he saw. Maybe it was just a man who felt the cold. But now it seemed that his suspicions were confirmed. He waved the severed lump of flesh in the air, and shrugged.

'It seems to point to the Tartars – who else would do this? Who else was here?'

As if in response to his question, a strange ululation echoed round the grim chamber. Bacon looked sharply at Falconer, and motioned him into silence with a finger to his lips. Soon they heard the sound again, this time more like a chant or incantation. Bacon pointed towards the rear door to the hall, and Falconer nodded. It certainly seemed to be coming from behind it. They both tiptoed over to the door, which stood slightly ajar, and listened intently at the crack. Though the chanting had stopped, Falconer thought he could now hear a shuffling sound, like the padding back and forth of some wild creature. He wondered if whatever it was behind the door had killed Brother Bernard, not a human agency after all. There was only one way to find out.

Gesturing at Bacon to stand back, he pushed the door open a crack, and peered round. He was looking into the kitchen, with a large open hearth at one end, and a scarred and grubby table in the middle. A line of dusty pots against one wall stood as mute testimony to the infrequent use of the room, and a second door in the right-hand wall probably led out into the rear yard. An unpleasant odour of stale fat hung in the air, mixed with a more rank aroma of a long unwashed body. At the table, knife in hand, stood a very old man with a long straggly beard. His dome of a head was liver spotted, and all but devoid of hair. The hands that held the knife between them were like claws, the knuckles no more than knobbly bones with veined parchment stretched over them. The ancient was trying to cut himself some bread, and muttering incoherently through slack and dribbling lips. His renewed and unconcerned caterwauling emboldened Falconer to swing the door fully open and step into the room. As he did so, the old man looked up, and cackled.

'Yet more visitors. Indeed, we are blessed today – there haven't been so many visitors since . . .'

He obviously couldn't recall a time that compared with this moment, and returned to his task of hacking the loaf of bread apart. He also began to mumble to himself under his breath, but Falconer could not make it out. Bacon spoke up from behind Falconer's shoulder, uncertainty in his voice:

'You don't think he could have killed the Dominican, do you?'

Falconer shook his head. 'Look at his hands, they are bent with the crippling disease. He can hardly hold a knife to cut bread, let alone hack an ear off.'

Bellasez came from behind the table, revealing dusty buskins with holes worn in them, through which poked the old man's toes. He shuffled past Falconer, and perched himself on a stool by the hearth. Apparently unaware of what had happened next door, he gnawed contentedly at the crust of bread with his toothless gums.

'Do you think he saw anything?' Bacon's doubtful question reminded Falconer what the old man had said when he first entered the room. He leaned casually against the wooden beam that topped the hearth, as though he had just dropped in for an exchange of gossip with the old man.

'So we're not the first visitors you've had today, then?'

Two rheumy eyes were turned on Falconer, indignation etched into them.

'Indeed not. Nor the most important – for who are you?' Before Falconer could offer their names, the old man pressed on. 'I will tell you – by the state of your clothes you're nothing more than a pair of impecunious scholars . . . And there's plenty of those in this town, I can tell you.'

Falconer smiled ruefully. Both he and Bacon did indeed dress shabbily – who could deny it? Though to be reminded of it by someone whose own clothes were no more than rags was rather irksome. The old man eagerly continued:

'Today, I have seen the Lost Tribe.'

The Lost Tribe? Falconer did not understand. Bellasez saw the confusion in his eyes, and spoke to him as to a child:

'The Lost Tribes of Israel – sent by God into exile in the East. They have come back, and he sent me for them. Get the Rabbi David, he said, and I did. He came here and heard the friar confess his sins.'

Realization dawned for Falconer. 'The Tartar priest, David – he came here?'

'Go to the Tartars, find the priest David, that's what he said. He said priest, but he meant rabbi. They are Israelites. Anyway, priest or rabbi, I brought him, and the friar confessed to him.'

'Confessed? To what?'

Bellasez irritatingly ignored Falconer's questions, and pressed on with his story.

'Then the other one came too. There was some scuffle, and the rabbi left.'

'The other one?' Falconer hoped he meant Guchuluk, but didn't want to jump to conclusions. 'You mean Sir Hugh?'

Bellasez looked quizzically at Falconer, not knowing the

name. So Falconer described Leyghton for him. Bellasez pulled a face in annoyance. 'No, no. He came later. No, I mean another of the Lost Tribe came.'

Bacon touched Falconer's arm and spoke quietly: 'Can he mean Guchuluk?'

'Probably – he was the only other Tartar who came into the city, as far as we know. But the old man thinks the Tartars are the Lost Tribes of Israel.'

'Then Guchuluk was definitely here – inside the Domus.'

Bellasez overheard this last remark. 'I said so, didn't I?'

Falconer could hardly believe that he had a witness to Bernard's murder, and eagerly posed the key question: 'And what did you see then, after the . . . rabbi had gone?'

The old man sniffed haughtily. 'I do not poke my nose into other people's business. I was here in the kitchen, and they were all in the hall.'

'Then how do you know the second visitor was a Tartar . . . another member of the Lost Tribe?'

Bellasez looked slyly at Falconer, and pointed at the door in the far corner of the room. Bacon went over and opened it, poking his head out to see where it led. He reported his findings to Falconer.

'You can see up the passage to the front door from here.'

The old man cupped his claw of a hand to his ear, obviously not able to hear clearly from across the room. Bacon spoke loudly for him:

'You saw him from here.'

Bellasez cackled, and nodded his head at the newly shared secret. 'I saw him all right, and I saw the other one – the blond-haired Christian – but he came later.'

'But you didn't see what happened in the hall?' muttered Falconer.

'Eh?' The old man raised his hand to his ear again.

'Nor hear what happened either,' concluded Bacon, staring glumly at the contented Bellasez. The sound of heavy footfalls in the adjacent room ended their fruitless interrogation of the senile old man. Sir Hugh had obviously returned with Peter Bullock. With no evidence to show that it had been anyone other than one of the Tartars, Falconer now had no way of stopping a very unpleasant incident taking place. At least he might persuade the constable to arrange its handling more delicately than Sir Hugh would choose. Falconer and Bacon returned to the grisly murder chamber, closing the kitchen door gently behind them.

'William.' Bullock was squatting over the huddled corpse, and turned a grim look on the two men as they entered the room. 'It would appear that my vigilance has not prevented the Tartars infiltrating the city, and doing incalculable harm.'

'And we should wipe them out now.' Leyghton's words may have echoed Peter Bullock's sentiment, but the constable was canny enough to know that rushing hot-headed into the Tartar camp was not a wise move. Straightening his stiffened limbs with the help of his scabbarded sword, he laid a firm hand on Sir Hugh's arm.

'Let me deal with this matter, my lord. I am appointed by the burgesses and aldermen of Oxford to uphold the law. And though I have no jurisdiction over the masters of this university, and must wait on the chancellor's pleasure – ' at these words he glowered at Falconer, who knew this restriction irked the constable – '. . .I can and will maintain the king's peace.'

Leyghton appeared to subside somewhat at this reassurance, and the invocation of the king's name. But he still did not fully give way. 'I will agree to you dealing with it. But the monster should hang for what he has done, and not be allowed to buy his freedom – ambassador or not.'

Bullock stood his ground. 'You have my word that the full force of the law will be invoked on the head of whoever did this deed.'

Leyghton nodded curtly. 'Then I will go and talk to Brother Adam about arranging a decent burial for Bernard.'

Once he had left the room, Bullock breathed a great sigh of relief, and looked warily at Falconer. 'I hope you aren't going to tell me it wasn't the Tartar, after all. For Sir Hugh will demand one of their heads, guilty or not.'

Falconer was about to speak, but it was Bacon who intervened:

'You know, this is all a matter of timing, and if only we could measure time itself more accurately, it would help us reveal who did this.' He waved a hand at the body at their feet, raising a cloud of flies that had settled on the drying blood spread in a pool across the floor.

Bullock looked puzzled. 'What do you mean?'

Bacon began to pace the floor as if he were lecturing to a room full of students, oblivious to the pool of sticky blood; his pacing took him ever closer to though never into it. Neither Falconer nor Bullock could take their eyes off his dangerous course, even as they listened to his thesis.

'We know that Brother Bernard had three visitors – the Tartar priest David, the other Tartar ...'

'Gutch-a-look.'

Bacon smiled at Bullock's mangled pronunciation. 'Guchuluk. And Sir Hugh himself.'

'You're not suggesting that Sir Hugh Leyghton did this!' Bullock was horrified at the idea.

Bacon tipped his head to one side in thought, and then continued, 'Now that you mention it – why should we not consider him? If we could only verify when the murder was committed, and when each of the three men was in the room with Bernard, it would be a simple matter to name the guilty party.'

Falconer sighed in disappointment – he had thought for a moment that his friend had a workable solution to the problem. 'If each of their visits were days apart, and if someone saw the victim alive in the mean time, perhaps this would be possible. But to be able to split time between, say, sext and nones into a finite number of measuring moments . . .' Falconer left the impossibility unspoken.

Bacon sighed deeply. 'You are right. For now.'

Before Falconer could ask him to qualify his assertion, Bacon took his leave of the two other men, claiming a pressing matter of scientific investigation. Left with a corpse which was beginning to stink in the hot and stuffy confines of the room, Bullock and Falconer stepped out into the relatively more salubrious air of the fish market. Though one or two curious glances were cast their way, the events of the past hour were already fading in the traders' minds. A bloodied man; the arrival of the constable; the departure of the bloodied man unrestrained – clearly nothing much had occurred. And if murder had been committed, it would only have been on the body of a Jew-convert. And what was less significant than such a sorry creature? Even Falconer quickly forgot Bellasez, the almost-witness to the murder. The question uppermost in his mind was put into words by Bullock:

'Is this connected to the murder of the old Tartar in any way, do you think?'

The constable used the epithet 'old' for anyone beyond their middle years, despite the fact he himself was well beyond the age of those he so described. Walking beside the constable as they negotiated the crowd, Falconer could not help but think Bernard's death was connected to Chimbai's, coming so hard on its heels. And involving the same suspects. He nodded in confirmation.

'Either Bernard saw who killed Chimbai, and the murderer knew this, and sought him out . . .'

Bullock broke in: 'Which would explain Bernard's fear, and desire to hide away.'

'. . . Or Bernard himself was the murderer, and Guchuluk sought to exact revenge on his own, without waiting for your good English justice to prevail. But – '

Bullock knew Falconer always found a *but* in any apparently straightforward proposition. He waited for the scholar to continue.

'If Bernard were the killer, and Guchuluk knew, why would he seek revenge when, according to Roger, he wanted Chimbai dead himself?'

'And the heretic priest?'

Bullock's reference to David troubled Falconer, for he hadn't seriously considered the priest as the murderer of Chimbai. He, of all of his fellow Tartars, seemed too afraid to have had the courage to do so. Still, if he were to talk to Guchuluk, he could at least sound out the interpreter at the same time. He was finding it difficult to understand what drove the Tartars, and it frustrated him. Then, for some reason, he suddenly recalled the plight of the elephant, languishing in the dingy stables of Oxford castle, and what Ann Segrim had said to him at their last meeting: *If we understood its life, we might be able to save it*. Perhaps if he really knew what these Tartars were like, he might understand the reason for Chimbai's death, and, as a consequence, Bernard de Genova's. No more Gog and Magog, or the Lost Tribes of Israel, or even the plague on mankind and anthropophagi. He had to see them as they were – ordinary human beings with the same weaknesses, lusts and desires as the people bustling around him in the market.

'Come, Peter. The time has come to find out the truth about these Tartars one way or the other.'

Fourteen

There on the mountains of Israel you shall fall, you, all your squadrons, and your allies; I will give you as food to the birds of prey and the wild beasts. You shall fall on the bare ground, for it is I who have spoken.

Ezekiel 39: 4–5

When Sir Hugh Leyghton returned again to the Domus Conversorum, he brought with him a stony-faced Adam Grasse and four Dominican brothers who could be trusted to keep what they saw a secret. Though the friars had been warned that Bernard's body had been defiled, they still were shocked by the sight that confronted them. The stench in the room was overpowering, and the flies that were disturbed by the men's entrance rose in an angry buzzing mass. The four brothers worked grimly at their task, wrapping the blood-stained body in a long white cloth, and bearing it sombrely out of the room on their shoulders. Brother Adam stared for a long time at the, by now, black stain on the hard clay floor, and the splashes that dotted the grubby wall. Suddenly he remembered there had been an inhabitant of this sorry place – an old man that Bernard had believed had cast off the Jewish faith and adopted Christianity. He would be in need of Christian charity now.

'Where is Bellasez?'

Sir Hugh did not understand. 'Who?'

'The old Jew-convert who lives here. Bernard doted on him, as his only success. Has no one thought to look for him?'

Sir Hugh's face exuded concern. 'I did not know there was anyone else here other than Bernard. No one said.'

Adam hurried through the door at the far end of the hall, and entered the kitchen. Leyghton heard his voice calling out, relief in his tone.

'It's all right. The old man is here, and he's fast asleep.'

Sir Hugh crossed to the low arched door, and looked on the skeleton of a sleeping man hunched up in the corner of the hearth. He was covered in dusty ashes that made his patched robe look as grey as his skin – so much so that he resembled a ghost.

'The poor man is very old,' explained Grasse. 'And probably didn't even know of Bernard's death. Or, if he did, it's gone from his mind already. I bless the forgetfulness of old age.'

'He looks as good as dead already,' opined Sir Hugh.

When Falconer and Bullock reached the Tartar camp, they saw nothing that would suggest Guchuluk was in fear of what their purpose might be. But then he had had plenty of time to prepare himself – the two Oxford men would have announced their arrival well in advance as they crossed the open meadow between the camp and the city. The flap of the tent formerly occupied by Chimbai was propped open, and a curl of smoke drifted lazily into the air from the opening in the top of the tent. Everything was arranged to suggest normality.

As the two men came closer, one of the soldiers, whom Falconer recognized as the man who had failed in his duty to guard Chimbai's life, stepped out of the tent. He motioned for Falconer and Bullock to stand where they were, and called back over his shoulder into the tent. After a while Guchuluk himself emerged, and waved the two men in with an apparently friendly gesture. They stooped to follow him into the tent, and were plunged into the darkness of the shady interior. When his eyes had adjusted to the gloom inside, Falconer could see that Guchuluk was lounging on the raised platform formerly occupied by Chimbai. He was obviously making sure everyone – visitor and subordinate – was aware of his new status. Beside him stood a nervous David, fidgeting with the cross that hung from his neck. Yeh-Lu and the other soldiers were nowhere to be seen, unless they skulked behind the brightly coloured rugs that hung from the roof of the tent, dividing it into separate compartments. In the momentary silence Falconer listened, but there was no sound from behind the drapes – everything indicated that Guchuluk was prepared for a private exchange of views. Falconer crouched down, making himself as comfortable as he could. Bullock remained standing near the entrance to the tent, a mirror image of the soldier standing guard outside.

Guchuluk looked relaxed, and spoke directly at Falconer in his guttural tongue. As ever, David translated.

'The Bahadur Guchuluk would offer you *kemiz*, but is not sure that your palate is subtle enough to appreciate its flavours.'

There was a smile on Guchuluk's lips as he listened to David's translation. Recalling Sir Hugh Leyghton's reaction, Falconer, too, smiled.

'Tell him that we should all refrain from *kemiz* at the moment, as we are going to require clear heads.'

David turned to relay the words to Guchuluk, and Falconer noticed a bead of sweat appear on the priest's upper lip, glistening through the sparse moustache. Indeed, as Falconer and Guchuluk traded polite compliments, the priest's face began to glisten, and his movements became more and more jerky, as though he were not truly in control of himself. Falconer wondered if he could last much longer under the scrutiny of both men's gazes. With the exchange of amenities at an end, Falconer finally approached the matter of Chimbai's death. He knew Guchuluk would be expecting it, and would have marshalled his thoughts already. So he began with an innocent question:

'Would you describe to me again what your men saw in the tent where Chimbai's body was?'

Guchuluk looked a little puzzled at the question, but, through David, answered it all the same.

'There was no one else in the tent, save for Chimbai. He lay before the images of the god Tengri and his family.'

'Could they have missed seeing someone – hidden behind Tengri, for example?'

On hearing the question translated, Guchuluk scoffed. 'The images of the gods are made of felt, and are not that big.'

Falconer pondered for a moment. 'How was the body found?'

'I do not understand your question,' stammered David, beads of sweat now springing up all over his face. 'The soldiers found him – you know that.'

'No.' Falconer strove to keep patient. 'I meant, in what position was he? On his back, or his front?'

David translated and the answer came back from Guchuluk.

'On his back.'

'What way round did the body lie?'

'With his head towards the tent opening.'

Now was the time to ask a more pertinent question.

'Were you angry that Chimbai was chosen over you to represent your nation to our king?'

Guchuluk snorted in disgust, and David translated his angry reply:

'It was only the last efforts at wielding power by the Berke family – their death-throes, if you like. Their heads are buried in the past, constantly retelling the old stories of Dua the One-eye. If they were to rule, we would be constantly fighting the old battles, and revenging the betrayal of Ambakkhai to the Golden Emperor. You call us Tartars, but we are Mongols and our ancestor Chinghis took revenge on the Tartar clan for his father's betrayal at the Ulkhui-Shilugeljit River more than fifty years ago.' Guchuluk's tone softened, and Falconer listened with interest, half to the sound of his voice, and half to David's translation.

'Now we must look forward – to trading and alliances. You call us beasts, but we can bring you many things – defeat of the Muhammadans, for one. The Great Khan, Kublay loves literature and science, especially of the Chin people – people like Yeh-Lu. You should see his winter palace at Cambaluc, the capital of Cathay – its walls are covered in gold and silver. It is enclosed by a wall four miles round, and inside it there is an enclosure within which there are parks and beautiful trees where deer, gazelles and animals that give musk live.' Guchuluk's eyes had taken on a distant look as he retold the marvels of the court he had only seen once as a youth, when taken there by his father. 'There is a hill made by art, on which stand hundreds of different trees, brought there bodily, roots and all, by Kublay's command. How does that make us beasts, and you so pure? Here, all I've seen is filth and smells. If we join with you, we can bring you turquoise stones, and silk embroidery from Kerman; pearls, and precious stones and spices from Hormos, as well as the sulphur cure for the itch and many other diseases; from Kamadi we can bring dates, pistachio nuts, and the apples of Paradise. Is this the work of monsters?'

The flat rendition of Guchuluk's words by David did not catch the impassioned intonations of the man, but Falconer understood him nevertheless. He was silent for a while, trying to remake his image of the Tartar in the light of the words he had just spoken. The young man presented a very different picture from the tales told of the Tartars, when Christendom had first encountered them barely thirty years earlier. And yet he still felt the contempt the young man had had for Chimbai, the old and drunken savage of a man who had been his superior. He still could be the killer – of the Noyan Chimbai and Bernard de Genova both.

Guchuluk stared at Falconer, knowing what was in the scholar's eyes. He let out a hiss of breath through his clenched teeth. Through David, he spoke curtly now.

'I see I need to have someone else convince you that I did not kill the noyan, much as I might have wished it, and was glad of it when it happened. For it made my task all that much easier.'

Casting a glance over his shoulder at the rug that formed a backdrop to where he sat, he called out in a different tongue from his own. Something stirred behind the drape, and Falconer could sense the constable tensing behind him. The old man would never really trust the Tartars, the demons incarnate of his years as a soldier. Falconer would have liked to think he was not going to be surprised at who emerged to stand at Guchuluk's shoulder, but he was. Having ascribed the role of avenger to the Templar, it was difficult to place Guillaume de Beaujeu at the Tartar's right hand. But there was no mistaking the Frenchman's impassive features as he spoke quietly to Guchuluk in a tongue the man clearly understood. In fact, harsh words were clearly being exchanged, albeit in subdued tones, until de Beaujeu turned back to look at Falconer.

'It is much against my better judgement that I have revealed myself to you here. And even more so that I am going to tell you what I am. But Guchuluk insists. He thinks it will rid him of your continual suspicions and interference into his affairs.' Falconer thought he detected a small grin flicker across the Templar's lips. 'Knowing you as I do, I fear it will not. But, I said I would try.'

As if suddenly aware of David's presence, Guchuluk put a hand on de Beaujeu's arm, and spat out a curt command to his interpreter. The priest paled, but bowed and stepped out of the tent into the late-afternoon sun. Allowing a few moments to pass, Guchuluk was obviously satisfied that the man was out of ear-shot, and made a sign for de Beaujeu to continue. By way of explanation, the Templar said that he and Guchuluk spoke together in the Turkish tongue, which they both understood. It had kept what they planned strictly between themselves.

'For it would not do for the rest of Christendom to know what the Grand Master plans as yet. Do you understand what I am saying?' He stared hard at both Falconer and Bullock. Both men understood perfectly – de Beaujeu would only help their enquiry if they kept their mouths shut about the Tartar and the Templar. A silent agreement was all that de Beaujeu needed, and he proceeded to explain why he was here. It appeared that he and Guchuluk had met in secret several times now, agreeing how the Tartars would aid the Templars in the Holy Land. Secrecy was essential at this stage of negotiations, for Count Bohemund had been excommunicated by the pope for just such an alliance.

'Then what is different now?' Falconer was curious to know how the Grand Master of the Templars would bring the pope to his way of thinking this time. De Beaujeu's eyes sparkled.

'You know the story of Prester John?'

Of course Falconer knew the ancient legend of Prester John. He was a mythical Eastern Christian prelate, who, at a time of crisis for Christendom, it was predicted, would emerge from the fastnesses and help liberate the Holy Land. It was nonsense – the stuff of children's bedtime stories. Did a sane man such as de Beaujeu really believe it?

'It matters not whether I believe it or not. The Grand Master has a letter – an ancient letter – purporting to come from the presbyter himself. It will convince the ignorant and the hopeful of his true existence. And now, when many Tartars are converting to Christianity, the mantle of Prester John can easily be hung around their shoulders.'

Falconer had always known there was something of the pragmatist about de Beaujeu. The Templar wasn't as gullible as his Grand Master, but he could see the value of allowing others to believe. So he didn't need any more convincing that what de Beaujeu said was true. All along, he had not been stalking the Tartars, but had been negotiating an alliance with the old Templar demon.

'I won't even remind you of the necessity of using a long spoon in such circumstances,' murmured Falconer. 'But tell me, how does this help my investigation into Chimbai's death?'

De Beaujeu smiled bleakly. 'Simple. Guchuluk was with me when Chimbai was killed. So he could not have been his murderer.'

'And Bernard de Genova?'

'What of him?'

'Where was Guchuluk when Bernard de Genova was killed?'

De Beaujeu grimaced, clearly not aware of the demise of Sir Hugh Leyghton's secretary. He shot a question in Turkish at Guchuluk. The Tartar's face reddened, but he shook his head in denial.

'He says he does not know this man – why are you accusing him of his murder?'

'He does not know him, yet he was seen in his house at the

time Bernard's throat was cut, and his ear chopped off. Does that not remind you of one of the Tartars' more endearing habits?'

Once again de Beaujeu taxed the Tartar in the tongue they shared, thus excluding Falconer from the conversation, much to his annoyance. He had taken Ann's indirect suggestion and tried to understand the Tartars, but he was still hampered by not speaking their language. As the conversation between the two men grew heated, Falconer became more and more anxious to hear the import of Guchuluk's words. He interrupted the Templar in mid-sentence:

'What is he saying?'

'If you'll allow me to finish, I will tell you.'

Guchuluk barked a further command, and de Beaujeu, though looking quizzical, translated for Falconer.

'He says he did go to the house of a black-clad man with a bald head – I suppose he means a tonsure – but he was only following the Nestorian priest to find out what he was doing.' De Beaujeu looked briefly at Guchuluk, who nodded, and gestured at Falconer, as if to say, get on with it. 'He asked the priest what he had told the shaven-headed man. Demanded he tell him, is a clearer translation. David told him the man – de Genova, I suppose – had asked him to listen, not talk. I think by 'listen' he means David heard de Genova's confession, though I cannot be sure. Then Guchuluk sent David back to camp. He was going to leave himself, but Genova grabbed his sleeve and gabbled something he could not understand. He says the man was incoherent most of this time anyway, muttering some sort of ritualistic chant under his breath.'

'And nothing happened?'

'He says he gave up trying to find out what David had been up to when he heard someone trying to open the street door.

He did not wish to be found in Oxford, so he left through the kitchen.'

Falconer thought immediately of Bellasez. 'Through the kitchen? Are you sure?'

De Beaujeu sighed, and asked Guchuluk a question. The Tartar nodded and added something in Turkish.

'He says, ask the old man who was there – he would have seen him.'

So at least Guchuluk knew of Bellasez, and his presence in the kitchen. That was reasonable proof of that part of his statement. But was de Genova dead by then? If Guchuluk were the killer, he wouldn't tell, and the senile Bellasez couldn't tell.

'He also says he waited until the visitor – whoever it was – had been admitted, before he left by way of the side alley.'

'Admitted? I suppose by saying that he hopes to suggest Bernard was still alive. But the visitor could have let himself in, and found Bernard dead. If Bellasez is to be believed, the next person to arrive was Sir Hugh Leyghton, and he found Bernard dead.'

Falconer had to wait in frustration again whilst de Beaujeu spoke to Guchuluk. This time he didn't really need a translation – Guchuluk spoke briefly, but his main response was an indifferent shrug of the shoulders.

'He says, maybe it was David at the door. Maybe he came back. Ask the old man.'

'Perhaps I should ask David first why he might want to kill Bernard. Let's get him back in here.'

De Beaujeu translated Falconer's request, and Guchuluk called out to the guard at the entrance to the tent. The reply was prompt, and worrying. It appeared that, after having slunk around the back of the yurt, where he was in a position to have overheard their conversation, David had last been seen hurrying towards the city.

He had found it very easy to gain access to the House of Converts. As dusk fell, there was always a lull in the habitual bustle of Oxford's streets. The shopkeepers had gathered up their wares, stored them inside the little shops that formed the lower floor of most of the houses on Fish Street, and closed the shutters, which, let down, doubled as counters during the day. If they were fortunate, they returned to their pliant wives, and a well-deserved supper. Those who had no wives, or wives who did not do their bidding, retired to the consolations of the nearest ale-house to spend what they had earned during the day. It was only later that the rowdy students thronged the streets, alleviating their boredom with a little mischief-making. And tonight, apparently, was going to be a night for mischief — the word had gone about.

For now, the street in which the Domus Conversorum stood was virtually empty of people, and those who were abroad paid no attention to the dark-clad figure who entered the building. They were used to seeing Dominicans come and go in their attempts to convert the Jews. Most thought it would be easier to just get rid of them — banish them from England's shores for good. Then they would also be rid of the Converts' House, the synagogue, and all the Christ-murdering Jews in their neighbourhood. But they understood the friars' desire to carry out God's work, and ignored their comings and goings at the house.

Once inside, he could smell the rank odour of blood. As he passed from room to room in his search, it seemed to follow him, as though it pervaded the whole house. Or perhaps it just hung in his own nostrils, and would never leave him wherever he went. He looked in the kitchen, but could not find what he sought. Returning to the hall, he skirted the dark stain that had spread across the uneven floor, fearful he might step into a still-damp pool of blood lurking in the cracks of the hard-packed clay. He went up the stairs cautiously, almost every step complaining at the weight he put on it. It was like a chorus of inhuman groans that he could not suppress, accompanying his every move through this house. But what he was there for had to be done, if he were not to be found out.

His grim resolve was weakened, however, when he got to the top of the stairs and was confronted by a spectre. The gaunt and fleshless face of Brother Bernard hovered in the dark before him. He gave an involuntary cry of alarm, before the flame of a candle resolved the skeletal shape into the less alarming reality of the old man, Bellasez – a tallow candle in his claw of a fist illuminating his features from below his chin. Without further thought, the intruder leaped up the final step, and swung his clenched fist wildly at Bellasez's head. There was a sickening crunch as his knuckles made contact with the frail egg-like shell of the skull, and the old man fell insensate at his feet.

Fifteen

They shall take no wood from the fields nor cut it from the
forest but shall light their fires with weapons. Thus they will
plunder their plunderers and spoil their spoilers.

Ezekiel 39: 10

Falconer and Bullock, now concerned for Bellasez's safety, pushed through the flap of the Tartar tent, and began to hurry across the darkening meadow towards the city and North Gate. Bullock's head was full of questions and he gasped them out as he strove to keep up with the long-legged regent master.

'Do you think this priest killed the Tartar, and then de Genova for some reason?'

'And what reason could that have been, do you think?' Falconer threw his response over his shoulder, hardly breaking his fast pace.

'Maybe Bernard saw him kill Chimbai, and he was silencing the only witness to his crime.'

Falconer stopped in his tracks, and frowned at the panting constable. 'It is difficult enough to place someone in the tent at the time of the murder, what with the three guards surrounding the tent. But to place Bernard as a witness thereabouts also . . .'

Falconer left the impossibility unspoken, and resumed his loping pace across the grassy meadow. Bullock pondered the problem for a while, then thought of an alternative solution to the mystery of David's disappearance. He hurried after Falconer.

'Maybe the Dominican killed Chimbai, and David killed him in revenge. He is supposed to have heard de Genova's confession, after all. He was so angered at learning of the murder, he slipped back into the house after he assumed Gutch-a-look had gone, and did away with the noyan's killer. Now he has learned that he might have left a potential witness to this second death in the house, and is on his way to eliminate him. Isn't that why you're in such a hurry? Admit it.'

Falconer grunted. 'Something like that, but I think . . .'

Bullock was not to know then what Falconer thought, because they were both distracted by a mass of bobbing lights streaming out of both North Gate straight ahead and Smith Gate to their left. The men were stopped in their tracks, and before Falconer could fumble his eye-lenses up to his face, Bullock saw what was afoot.

'Someone has shoved a stick into the wasps' nests that are your students halls, and stirred it around.'

With the lenses to his eyes, Falconer could see that the bobbing lights were flaming torches held by a mob of young men, advancing on the Tartar encampment. They were mainly dressed in the drab homespun of the poorer students, who would do anything for a few coins and a drink. But Falconer could also discern the odd brightly coloured gown of some noble's son. They got involved in trouble just for the hell of it. As the mob approached, their incoherent cries soon resolved into individual demands for the expulsion of the 'beasts and monsters' that besmirched their fields. At close quarters, both men could see that most of the students carried weapons – mainly staves and clubs – but a few swords were also apparent. One youth, prominent at the head of the mob, was carrying a bow.

'You are right,' muttered Falconer. 'Someone has stirred them up, and I know who. This is the work of the chancellor.'

'De Ewelme? Why?'

'He said he was going to rid himself of the Tartars somehow. Remember I told you there was a man of some power, whom I feared had been intent on killing a Tartar. Someone whose name it was better you didn't know. It was de Ewelme I feared had done something stupid, with the involvement of a student called Miles Bikerdyke – a good archer, I was told.' He looked hard at the bow-carrying youth. 'It seems I gave the chancellor too much credit. His wasn't a devious plan to kill Chimbai, but simply to stir up our little wasps' nest, and cause a few painful bites.'

'And some of the wasps will get swatted while they are about it.'

Bullock, who counted the student mob at no more than half a hundred, still didn't doubt that the handful of battle-hardened Tartar soldiers would be more than a match for them. Most of the students were aroused by drink, no doubt, and would flee at the first sign of a violent and co-ordinated response to their disorganized protest. But he was worried about the handful of lethal weapons in the students' midst. An inexpertly flighted arrow from a drunken student could still kill, and carnage would then follow. He grabbed Falconer by the arm.

'You go and see if you can deal with the priest. I'll sort these fools out.'

By now the students were on top of the two men, buffeting them as they marched past. Falconer and Bullock stood as if bracing themselves against the pull of a swiftly flowing stream. Falconer could see the nervous look in some of the youths' eyes as they passed, and nodded in response to Bullock's suggestion. If any one man could stop them in their tracks, it was the constable, who was already sizing up who were the ringleaders. First, he would deal with them swiftly and harshly, and then the others would melt away. He hoped.

Falconer wished him luck. 'At least we can strike de Ewelme from our list of suspects for the noyan's murder. This rabble is clearly all he can effectively organize.'

He patted the old man on his bowed back, and pushed his way through the stragglers. Bullock followed his passage for a moment, then spat on his hands and rubbed them together. Loosening his trusty sword in its scabbard, he lumbered after the student ringleaders, a gleam in his watery eyes. Forget murder and all its convolutions, this was work he could relish.

The House of Converts had been placed provocatively by the king in the centre of the area known as Jewry, with Jews' homes ranged on either side, and facing it across Fish Street. Indeed the house, situated close to Carfax, had once belonged to Joseph, son of Isaac, who had converted and taken the name of Alberic Convers. It was of some consolation to the Jews who lived in its proximity that the house, in comparison to their own, was shabby and run down, being so very little used. Old Jehozadok, the unofficial patriarch of the Oxford Jews, lived close by at the synagogue, only a few doors away. He deeply regretted ignoring the needs of Bellasez when his daughter, Saphira, had died. They had played together as children in Spain before their respective families had sought the relative security of England. Once settled in Oxford, he and Bellasez had drifted apart, as the latter pursued his father's profession of usury, and became more and more cantankerous and argumentative, and Jehozadok adopted the mantle of rabbi. They had argued bitterly when Jehozadok had attempted to come to Bellasez's aid on Saphira's first falling ill of the fever. Bellasez had asserted his independence then, and the result was that Jehozadok had stayed away when the old man had needed him most. When Saphira died, it had been a source of scandal in the introspective community that Bellasez had thrown himself upon the mercies of the Christians and moved into the Domus.

Now that Jehozadok had heard that the Dominican who ran the Domus had been killed, he feared for Bellasez, and was determined to help the old man, whether he liked it or not. He smiled at his own characterization of Bellasez as 'the old man' – their ages, after all, were exactly the same. But even as a child, the scrawny Bellasez had seemed old before his time, thin and solemn in appearance. He had simply spent the last half century growing into the role he now occupied.

Leaning heavily on the stout stick that served both as a support and as a weapon, should he be accosted, Jehozadok made his wary way along the rubbish-strewn street towards the Domus. He would not have normally ventured out at such a time, preferring the security of his stone-built home, and its firm, oak front door. But the news of the death of the Dominican had only just been brought to him, and he didn't want to delay a second time over bringing succour to Bellasez. He did wish that he had summoned someone younger to assist him, though. His sight was not all it should be, and he was afraid of tripping and breaking his brittle old bones. Still, it was not far to go, and then he would be able to rescue Bellasez – from himself.

He was just crossing the end of Jewry Lane, a dark, narrow passage running off Fish Street, which cut the eastern part of Jewry in two, when a dark figure appeared out of the gloom. The tall and intimidating person almost knocked him off his feet as he brushed past, and turned down the passage without speaking. Jehozadok stumbled, and only kept on his feet by thrusting his stick out in front of him. He stood in this awkward posture for a while, breathing deeply, his heart thumping. He was unable to recover his balance properly at first. Had it been a deliberate attack, or had it been an accident that the man had not felt it necessary to apologize for? He certainly had had no sight of the man's face, which had been hooded.

Eventually his legs stopped trembling and his heart ceased pounding. Then he pushed himself upright, and continued on his uncertain way, hurrying as fast as his shaky legs would take him. He was relieved when at last he saw the door of the Domus, and dragged himself up the worn, broken steps. He went to knock at the door, and it was only then that he realized it was ajar. He cautiously pushed on the handle, and the door swung back ominously. No one in Jewry – even a convert – would leave his door unbarred at this late hour. Many an incautious Jew had received a thrashing for having the temerity to live in England and keep his door unbarred. Jehozadok's heart started pounding again. He clenched his stick as firmly as his gnarled hands would allow, and stepped into the darkness beyond the door, calling out fearfully as he went:

'Bellasez. Are you there? It's me, Jehozadok.'

There was no reply, and the house felt cold. So cold.

Bullock drew his battered sword and strode after the rearguard of the student mob. The edge of the sword was no longer sharp and well-honed, as it had been in his soldierly days. Indeed, it was jagged and snaggle-toothed, with notches all along its length. But that didn't matter – Bullock normally brought only its broad, flat surface into use these days. Swung lustily across someone's arse, it was a salutary and stinging reminder of who was in charge in Oxford. Across someone's skull, it would quieten the more recalcitrant of offenders, who would next wake up in the constable's uncomfortable and smelly cell at the foot of St George's Tower with a powerfully sore head.

He thrust the blade between the pretty mincing legs of some extravagantly dressed youth, whose lack of desire for the physical aspects of an affray had kept him well to the rear of the mob. The boy tripped and fell, bloodying his nose on the hard ground. Bullock grunted in satisfaction as the blood spurted all over the youth's bright green doublet with its fashionably slashed sleeves, ruining it. He stepped over the ashen-faced youth and went in pursuit of another knot of back-markers. Swinging his blade judiciously from left to right, he soon reduced the number of agitators by a dozen or so, as shamefaced and sore-arsed youths scuttled away. He was now amongst the core of the mob, and knew these would be harder to deflect from their purpose. He would have to seek out the ringleader, and deal with him. Then the rest would soon disperse before they encountered less considerate opposition in the form of the Tartar soldiers.

At the head of the mob, illuminated by the torches held aloft by others, strode a tall, well-built youth with greasy, lank hair. As he turned to encourage those around him, Bullock saw he had an eruption of boils around his neck and chin that made his jaw look raw in the flickering light. But, more importantly, he was holding a bow in his left hand, an arrow already held in place with his crooked finger. Bullock growled, and tried to push his way through the jeering students. But the more he elbowed them aside, the more they jostled him, and he could see the raw-faced youth at their head pulling the bow-string back. The constable swung the flat of his sword left and right, careless of whether he broke skin or bone, but it was like ploughing through a tangled thicket. He saw the tremor of tension in the youth's elbow as he held the bowstring taut. Out of the corner of his eye, he saw a movement at the entrance to the biggest of the two remaining Tartar tents – the one he and Falconer had just recently left. A stooping figure emerged from the tent. Bullock saw it was Guchuluk, and he cried out a warning. The youth let go of the bowstring, and the arrow flew on its way.

Falconer was not sure what he might find in the House of Converts. The two mysterious deaths still had puzzling aspects to them, which seemed to point down blind alleys. If he could only find David and stop him from doing anything foolish, he felt he might begin to extricate himself from this maze. There were several pertinent questions he wanted to ask of a number of people, and then he might be in a position to substantiate his suspicions. For now, they were nothing more than that – suppositions based on an incomplete collection of truths, some of which conflicted with each other. For now, he would have to be content with protecting the life of one of his more unreliable witnesses.

Hurrying across Carfax, he almost collided with a scrawny child who scuttled under his feet like the rats that infested La Boucherie, the end of the High Street where the butchers plied their trade. He grabbed the child's tattered shirt and pulled him round. Like the rats, the child had obviously been scavenging for the scraps of fat and bone that the butchers left behind them. He was carrying a sack whose dubious contents stank, but he clutched it to his bosom as though it were full of gold. He turned his weasely face towards Falconer, then spat at the startled scholar. Shocked, Falconer let the urchin go, and watched as he scurried off into the darkness like any other rodent.

Falconer shook his head sadly, and, wiping his face clean, crossed Carfax to the top of Fish Street where the House of

Converts stood. The door was wide open, and he stepped cautiously in, listening for the slightest sound. For a moment he could hear nothing, then an eerie keening pierced the silence. It came from the top of the stairs, and Falconer leaped up the rickety structure towards the sound, fearful of what he might find. What he had not expected was to encounter Jehozadok, but the kneeling figure at the top of the stairs was the rabbi, without a doubt. He was bent over a bundle in his arms, his head thrown back, and his features set in a mask of despair. As his keening wail cut Falconer to his heart, the regent master realized that Jehozadok was cradling Bellasez's head in his gnarled hands. And the bald, mottled pate was covered in blood.

Sixteen

They shall go through the country, and whenever one of
them sees a human bone he shall put a marker beside it,
until it has been buried in the Valley of Gog's Horde. So no
more shall be heard of that great horde, and the land will be
purified.

Ezekiel 39: 15–16

The day dawned already hot and humid. An evil humour seemed to hang over Oxford, filling the air with a heaviness that sat oppressively on everyone's shoulders. A layer of haze enveloped the town like a blanket, holding the stench of nightsoil, rotting food and unwashed bodies in the narrow lanes and alleys. Not a breath of wind stirred the stinking brew, and the noxious airs filled the nostrils, and lodged stickily in the chest. Even the sewage channels that ran down Oxford's main streets seemed to be choked and turbid, the gutters hardly carrying out their function of conveying the town's wastes into the river and away. It was all conducive to bad temper and bitter argument, and though the sun was barely over the battlements Stephen Wytton, a goldsmith, had already beaten his wife senseless because she spilled ale on his new cap. And Gerard de Somerby, a sophister at the university after two years of study, had plunged a knife into the fleshy upper arm of a fellow student at Little Black Hall in Schools Street, because he had disputed the truth of de Somerby's assertion that a line is made up of a number of unextended points. Taking the view of Bishop Grosseteste that the opposite was true may have been old-fashioned, but it did not warrant such a murderous attack. Fortunately de Somerby's opponent in sophistry lived to share a drunken revel with him that same evening. Stephen Wytton's wife had to stay indoors and away from the prying eyes of neighbours until the bruises subsided.

For William Falconer, the morning was to bring unusual clarity, though it had not seemed like that at the onset. He had been lying awake, tossing and turning in the oppressive heat, and thinking of all that had happened recently. Most of all he thought of Bellasez. If only he had not been held up by the student mob, he might have been in time. However, one matter had resolved itself as a result of de Ewelme's little diversion. It had come about when Bullock had come to him the previous evening after he had returned, disconsolate, to Aristotle's Hall, and insisted he accompany him back to the Tartar camp.

He was not in the mood for mysteries, but the constable would not tell him why he had to leave the city in the dead of night for the uncertain pleasures of the northern meadows. When they got there, the perimeter of the camp was guarded by a stony-faced Sigatay and his men. No more foolish students were going to disturb Guchuluk and his entourage, and it was only by dint of some vigorous hand gestures and hard stares that Bullock got them through to the main tent. Then Falconer understood. An arrow had been fired during the riot – by Miles Bikerdyke, whom Bullock now had in his cell – and it had lodged in the Tartar tent, missing Guchuluk by a fair margin.

'Look,' said Bullock, pointing at the arrow embedded in the hard, blackened felt of the tent. It hung limply where it had struck, the head having gone through the material, but with most of the shaft still visible. 'There is no way that an arrow fired from the outside could have penetrated this material and still have had enough force to kill Chimbai. It must have been fired through the opening, and that means Sigatay must have been lying. He must have seen the archer . . . or been the archer.'

Bullock looked at Falconer in triumph at solving the mystery. But, by now, Falconer was deep in thought, and appeared to have ignored his friend's last comment. Not that he had by any means – he was merely trying to recall something he had been told about Chimbai's body. Something that didn't square with what Bullock was surmising. Something he had been told, which at the time he had thought inconsequential. Taken with the new information about the arrow's trajectory, it pointed to a greater truth. If only he could remember what it was.

Now, back in his solar in the early morning, the puzzle buzzed around his head like an annoying house fly, constantly distracting him, and preventing him from ordering his thoughts logically. Suddenly it came to him: Guchuluk had unwittingly revealed the truth when he had told Falconer how Chimbai's body was found before it was brought out of the tent. This fact, and the impossibility of an arrow being able to penetrate the material of the tent, did away once and for all with the theory of a superhumanly accurate archer standing far off. But, this being so, the maddening question returned of how someone had got into and out of the tent without being seen. It demanded that he ask a whole lot more questions, or it would remain there, mocking everything he had assumed until now about Chimbai's death – and everything that had happened since. He lay back on the bed, his head cupped in his clasped hands, and stared at the cracked and dusty ceiling. The only conclusion he could come to with the facts he had available was impossible to conceive of, and it brought to mind Bacon mocking the falseness of his 'all murderers are bloodied' syllogism.

Fortunately, his disordered and feverish thinking was disturbed by a youthful messenger who told him that 'his favourite student' awaited his tutelage. More than a little puzzled, and befuddled by the oppressive heat of the new day, he had asked where, and indeed who, this student might be. The youth's eyes twinkled, but he refused to be drawn on the identity of the person whose strange message he was carrying. He said that all he was allowed to say was that it concerned 'the great beast'. Realization dawned for Falconer, and he quickly donned his robe and boots and trotted across the wakening city to where the elephant was stabled.

The smell of the hot and windless city had been strong, but as soon as he came into the vicinity of the stables below St George's Tower, he was aware of a terrible odour that assailed the senses and churned the stomach. It was the scent of death, and, though it was enough to drive him away, Falconer took a deep breath, opened the stable door and stepped inside. Ann Segrim, apparently undeterred by the smell, knelt before the inert bulk of the great beast, stroking the long trunk that stretched out before her. The last time Falconer had seen the elephant it had been weak, its breathing stertorous. Now the flesh had shrunken on the massive frame, so that every ponderous bone was visible. Barely a whisper of breath disturbed the straw that lay around its mouth, but it was still alive. Ann turned round and there were tears in her eyes.

'I am glad you still consider yourself my favourite student. I had thought your course of study had come to an end.' Falconer stood over Ann, awkward and embarrassed. She smiled up at him weakly.

'I think there is still much for me to learn.'

Falconer responded gruffly. 'And for me. I only wish you were free to . . . pursue your studies more frequently. But I know you have duties as Humphrey's wife, and you cannot be in two places at once.'

Ann sighed. 'Would that I could. Perhaps I can make time stand still.'

It was then Falconer suddenly had the answer to his impossible question, and he marvelled at why he had not seen it before. He knew then who had killed Chimbai, and it only remained to draw a confession out of the man's lips. He thought of the strategies that were open to him, swiftly discarding the one Bullock might have favoured of a good beating. A scholar required a more subtle approach, and he recalled mention of the Tartar *mangudai* – the suicide troops who lured Christendom's knights to their doom. Then he knew what he had to do.

Ann Segrim recognized the faraway look in Falconer's eyes, and knew better than to disturb him. Falconer hated his train of deduction being broken, and with their friendship only newly mended, she dared not try its strength. In the end it was the dying beast that, in its innocence, broke the spell. A great sigh escaped the lips of the elephant, and William and Ann both looked down at it.

'There really was no hope for it, you know,' he murmured. 'Out of its proper place in nature, it was nothing more than a freak.'

'I hope you are referring to the elephant, and not us as master and student.'

Falconer cast a startled look at Ann, and guffawed when he saw a twinkle in her eye. She joined in his laughter, then moved towards the door, stepping gracefully through the filth.

'Now I must go, before Humphrey's steward wonders why it is taking even me so long to choose a new silver ring.'

'And I must speak to Roger Bacon about what he has hidden in that tower of his.'

Ann Segrim frowned. 'Talking science? I thought you were intent on unearthing the killer that is loose in Oxford.'

Falconer smiled secretively. 'I am.'

A cooling breeze blew along the river Thames and in through the window arch of Roger Bacon's tower room. So, though the same breeze brought with it the sickly sweet smell of the raw sewage that ran into the river from the town, the room was a comfortable retreat from the heat of the day for Falconer. He sat back on Bacon's narrow cot, wiping the sweat from his brow. Bacon, as usual, was up to his elbows in papers that lay scattered around him on his rickety table. Each time he leaned forward to search for another document, the table creaked ominously and threatened to tip Bacon and his precious papers unceremoniously on to the floor. Each time, he leaned back and no disaster occurred. The whole room seemed a chaos of confusion to Falconer, but Bacon appeared to be able to lay his hands on precisely what he wanted.

'Listen to this.' He produced a single sheet of parchment from under a pile at his left hand. 'I copied it from notes handed me by Robert the Englishman:

The method of making such a clock would be this, that a man make a disc of uniform weight in every part so far as possibly could be done. Then a lead weight should be hung from the axis of that wheel, so that it would complete one revolution from sunrise to sunrise, minus as much time as about one degree rises according to an approximately correct estimate.'

Bacon snorted. 'Approximately! The man is evidently no mathematician or he would not use such an abhorrent term as approximately.'

'But this horologium device – this clock. Can it truly be made?' asked Falconer.

'Can it? Of course. I have made it. Didn't I tell you? It does not work now, because the crucial part – the wheel – is missing. You were here when I told you I had lost it and could not get a replacement.'

He gestured towards the structure that stood in the gloomiest corner of his room, relegated to obscurity now it no longer functioned. It was a curious tangle of toothed wheels, etched dials and cords, suspended on a crude metal frame. Bacon preferred to call it his 'astrarium', claiming it could predict the course of the sun and moon, or the fixed stars, and foretell the rise and fall of the tides.

'If only I could get another wheel made, I could show you how I can also make it ring a bell as regularly as vespers in a monastery.'

Falconer smiled in quiet satisfaction. 'That is what I hoped you would say. And it leads me to suggest another experiment to you.'

Bacon listened with mounting curiosity as Falconer expounded his theory, and how Bacon could help him prove it. When Falconer finished speaking, Bacon paused for a moment, then nodded.

'I will do it.'

'Good. Now you must excuse me – I have to speak with someone else, and urgently.'

The room in Torold's Lane carried the unsavoury aromas of previous occupants, some of whom, it seemed, could not control their bladders. As Guillaume de Beaujeu's asceticism had its limits, and he no longer needed to hide away, he decided to clear his head in the open air. His aimless wanderings took him along the top of the city walls towards East Gate as he tried to catch the transitory breeze that wafted across from the River Cherwell on Oxford's eastern boundary. What he had been asked to do was curious in the extreme, and he could not fathom the reasoning behind it. This was most irksome to him, as he was used to controlling and shaping events himself, not being the pawn in someone else's chess game, whose strategy he could not understand.

He sighed and leaned on the rough stone of the battlements, feeling the warmth embedded there by the day's hot sun on his bare arms. He still wasn't sure if he was betraying the Grand Master and the risk he had been entrusted with. Once again he pulled the two documents from his pouch. The old one crackled under his fingers and he reread the text, though he could almost recite it without looking, so many times had he unfolded it:

By the power and virtue of God and the Lord Jesus Christ, King of Kings, know I am the greatest monarch under the Heavens. Seventy-two kings are under my rule, and my empire extends to the three Indias, including Farther India, where lies the body of Saint Thomas. In my dominions are the unclean nations whom Alexander Magnus walled up amongst the mountains of the North, and who will come forth in latter days . . .

His eyes dropped to the end of the ancient text.

Prepare for my coming.

If the Grand Master truly believed that the Tartars were the armies of Prester John, then who was he to cavil? And it was true that many of the great leaders in the Tartars' extended empire were baptized Christians. If they wished to enlist the aid of the Templars in crushing the Saracen armies in the Holy Land, then their goals were complementary, ringing true to the legend of Prester John. De Beaujeu's conversations with Guchuluk had almost borne fruit, and now what Falconer had asked him could jeopardize it all. He had thought of showing Falconer the second document the Grand Master had entrusted to him. It would have saved a deal of time, but he was not empowered to show it to anyone, unless it would serve as a bargaining counter in the last resort. He opened it slowly, as though fearful of letting a demon out of a bottle. It was a translated copy of a letter intercepted in Cyprus. It had been intended for someone in Chimbai's entourage, but the courier had died under clumsy torture before revealing to whom he was entrusted to deliver the letter. Its text was much more terse than the Prester John letter:

I am sending this letter by two different routes to ensure you receive this instruction. One at least should get to you in time. Know that Chimbai is allied with Mangku-Temur of the Golden Horde in support of Kaidu. If they should strengthen their position in the east, then Kublay could be in danger. Abaka has empowered us to do all that we can to stifle this alliance . . . so make sure that Chimbai does not return alive from England. I repeat in case the order is not clear enough for you – Chimbai must die.

No matter how many times he had read it, de Beaujeu could not extract from the words any sense of whom it had been intended for. That the other copy of the letter had got through to its intended recipient was testified to by Chimbai's death. Now Falconer reckoned he knew who it was had killed the Tartar, and had craved de Beaujeu's assistance in exposing him. The Templar just hoped it was not Guchuluk.

Falconer watched as they dragged the great beast out of the barn in which it had died. It took ten men to load it on a hurdle and pull it along Great Bailey. There had then ensued an argument as to whether it should be dragged openly through the market in Fish Street and so out of South Gate, or into Pennyfarthing Lane and surreptitiously out of the little gate in the south wall of the city. This gate had been cut by the Franciscan brothers of the friary outside the walls, and was their private way to and fro. It was not until Falconer pointed out that the bulky body would not fit through the Franciscans' gate, made as it was for human beings, that the matter was settled. The elephant would go out through South Gate in full view of everyone. In the end, there had been hardly anyone to witness the procession. Crowds had seen the beast enter the university city, but only the curious and the idle passer-by saw its exit. A deep pit had been dug below the walls, the bottom of it now filled with muddy water because of the low-lying situation. The interment had been ordered by Peter Bullock, as the massive body had begun to putrefy in the hot and sticky weather, carrying stinking odours up to Bullock's own chamber. At first the elephant-keeper had refused, as though by not carrying out this final act, he could stave off the fact of its demise. He would certainly have some difficulty explaining the loss of his charge to the king, but possessing a rotting body would not help in any case. Finally, gagging on the stench, Bullock had simply taken matters into his own hands, and had ordered the town grave-diggers to excavate a pit of the dimensions required. More used to the lesser proportions of a human body, they had toiled at their task for most of the previous day. Now, in the early hours of the following morning, the beast was tumbled into the hole. There it lay wallowing in the muddy bottom – a parody of its behaviour in life. Bullock paid off the pall-bearers, who were unlikely to officiate at such a strange funeral again, then he and Falconer left the grave-diggers to their grumblings, and the unpleasant task of shovelling the earth back over the mound of rotting flesh.

'A depressing business.'

Bullock had expected the burial of the beast to add to Falconer's woes. The Nestorian priest had disappeared as if by magic, and the murder hunt had apparently come to a dead halt. But, perversely, Falconer seemed almost cheerful. Bullock wanted to know why.

'Anyone would think you knew where the priest was.'

Falconer smiled enigmatically. 'I do.'

Bullock exploded in frustration at his friend's calm assertion:

'Then tell me, and I will take him. I am not afraid of the Tartars, you know. Once David is under lock and key in the tower, his comrades can howl at the city gates like the scavenging dogs they are. They will not gain admittance.'

'I will tell you where he is, I promise. But first he has to play his part in a little experiment I have arranged.'

'And the purpose of this experiment?' Sullen doubt that this experiment would serve any useful purpose was clear in Bullock's every word.

'Why, to furnish you with all the proof you need about the recent murders, of course.'

Seventeen

Come, assemble, gather from every side to my sacrifice, the great sacrifice I am making for you on the mountain of Israel.

Ezekiel 39: 17

The Dominican friary had not seen such activity since it had first been built and occupied twenty years before. Standing hard by Grandpont, it had often witnessed the comings and goings of lord, bishop and monarch from a distance, but today it was to host a unique assembly. Representatives of Christendom were to meet with those of the heathen Tartars to talk of alliances under the sponsorship of the Order of the Poor Knights of the Temple, guardians of the Holy Land. Guillaume de Beaujeu had laboured hard to get the agreement of all those who were to attend. Guchuluk had reluctantly agreed – he was still eager, despite the difficult circumstances, to forge alliances. That Nicholas de Ewelme, to be accompanied by Falconer himself, had taken no persuading was no surprise. The chancellor of the university would not have absented himself from such a table for the world. Curiously, it had been Sir Hugh Leyghton who was the most reluctant, even though he was charged with treating with the Tartars on behalf of King Henry. De Beaujeu had put it down largely to the intelligence from Templar spies that King Henry and his son were at loggerheads over the Tartars. The old man would have nothing to do with them, while Edward saw them as useful allies in Christendom's vain attempts to stem the disastrous loss of territory in Outremer. The Templar assumed that Sir Hugh was left in a quandary as to how to behave. The knight had at first argued he could not meet with men, one of whom was the murderer of his former secretary, Bernard de Genova. The Templar had had to use all his persuasive powers to convince Sir Hugh that nothing was proven, and, if his accusations did turn out to be true, the killer would not escape justice. Sir Hugh's second cavil — that he had no secretary — was quickly resolved by appointing one of Adam Grasse's friars to the position. A thin and scholarly man, of middle years, he gave the reassuring impression that he would perform his task with accuracy and humility. Thus armed, the knight, though grumbling at the imposition, was brought to the negotiating table with the Tartar bahadur, Guchuluk, accompanied this time by the man from Cathay, Yeh-Lu, and two of his guards. Only Falconer knew that Yeh-Lu spoke English, and de Beaujeu accordingly presented himself as interpreter, depending on his and Guchuluk's mutual understanding of the tongue of the Turks. David, of course, was still missing as far as everyone present was concerned.

As he oversaw everyone's arrival, the Templar puzzled over what Falconer hoped to achieve by this meeting. For though de Beaujeu had assumed the role of instigator, he had only acted on Falconer's request. The scholar, however, was clearly not interested in the grand plans of those who sat around the table, more in their peccadilloes which might reveal who was a murderer. But how he was going to winkle them out was still a mystery to de Beaujeu. He was already beginning to wonder if anyone was going to talk at all.

Sir Hugh Leyghton had glowered at Guchuluk when the Tartar contingent was ushered into the stark room that normally served as the refectory for the friary, and now studiously ignored him. The room still smelled of the friars' morning repast, and de Beaujeu's stomach grumbled at the enticing aroma of fresh wastel bread and pottage. His own breakfast had consisted of coarse rye bread and thin beer. He had to rouse himself from his dreams of good food when, recalling his role as interpreter, he heard Guchuluk offer a formal greeting to Henry's ambassador. He translated the words, but Sir Hugh's response was no more than a grunt. Unperturbed, Guchuluk sat down at the refectory table, with Yeh-Lu and his guards remaining standing close behind him. Sir Hugh pointedly sat at the opposite end of the long table, keeping the greatest distance he could from the Tartars. Finally, de Ewelme bustled into the room, apologizing for the absence of Regent Master Falconer, who, it appeared, had other business in the friary and would attend shortly. He was red-faced at such a lack of respect from the regent master, but had had no choice other than to leave him to his mysterious errand if he were to arrive on time himself. De Ewelme was eager to establish his position in the university town, and was petrified that the meeting would start without him, indicating his insignificance in the eyes of those present. He need not have worried – de Beaujeu was having great difficulty in getting Sir Hugh Leyghton even to speak. In lieu of any meaningful dialogue, de Beaujeu himself summarized the positions of both parties as he saw them, stretching out the meandering monologue with meaningless formalities. Having nearly exhausted his repertoire, and having repeated it in both English and Turkish for the benefit of both sides, he was silently cursing Falconer for putting him in this position and then failing to appear, when suddenly, behind him, the refectory doors swung open.

De Beaujeu could tell, even before he looked round, that Falconer had done something startling. He could see thunder clouds rolling across Sir Hugh's face, and his whole body was tensed. Even Guchuluk's normally impassive features betrayed his mystification as his eyes narrowed. Sir Hugh half-rose and cried out in strangled tones.:

'Are you going to fill this room with murderers?'

Wearily, the Templar looked over his shoulder. Falconer stood in the doorway with a pallid Tartar priest at his elbow. David was markedly reluctant to enter, and Falconer held him firmly by the arm. The priest nervously scanned the men seated around the long trestle table, his eyes betraying his fear of each and every one there. Ushered forward by Falconer, he stumbled into the room, looking as though he might vomit up whatever repast he had last eaten. He allowed himself to be seated next to Beaujeu, and swallowed hard. Guchuluk gave him a long, hard look, before staring pointedly at de Beaujeu. He obviously thought this was some incomprehensible strategy on the part of the English to embarrass him, and looked to the Templar for an explanation. De Beaujeu only wished he knew what strategy was being played out here, and looked pleadingly at Falconer. The regent master had placed himself between Nicholas de Ewelme and Sir Hugh Leyghton, though the space barely accommodated his bulky frame. In the process, he had managed to ease Sir Hugh back down on to the bench.

'Please excuse my tardiness, gentlemen. Only I chanced upon David in the cloister, and prevailed upon him to join us. He took some persuading, I fear.'

De Beaujeu was willing to bet that the last thing Falconer had done was 'chanced upon' the Tartar priest. He must have worked out that he had sought refuge at the friary. Though whether he should do so for fear of being accused of murder, or for another reason, the Templar did not know. Falconer answered his unspoken question immediately.

'Some think David guilty of the murder of the Dominican, Bernard de Genova, at the House of Converts. Though some . . .' And here he turned his innocent gaze on Sir Hugh, on his right. 'Some think that may be laid at the door of Bahadur Guchuluk.'

There was no need for de Beaujeu to translate for Guchuluk – he seemed to know precisely what Falconer was saying. His slit eyes bore into Sir Hugh, defying him to voice the accusation out loud. Falconer could feel Sir Hugh stirring at his side, and deliberately leaned against the poniard that hung at the knight's left hip.

'David, on the other hand, has something to tell us that will shed new light on Bernard's death . . . and perhaps on the death of Chimbai also.'

A rumbling sound escaped Sir Hugh's lips, though it was difficult to say whether it was provoked by anger or by another sort of emotion entirely. Guchuluk cast a questioning glance at de Beaujeu, as he was now lost as to what was happening, and desired a translation. As de Beaujeu leaned over and muttered in the Tartar's ear, David began his stammering and uncertain recital.

'It all began with the arrival of him who I now know as the Jew-convert Bellasez. I was not sure that the old man, when he came to our camp, really wanted me. He seemed confused over what he should call me, but I was persuaded to follow him back to the house where he lived. There I discovered it was I who was wanted. I found the man who had sent for me – Brother Bernard. He wanted to make a confession, and, for whatever reason, could not make it to those of his own order . . .'

'A confession about the murder of the Tartar, no doubt.' Sir Hugh seemed eager to conclude David's story for him.

The Nestorian priest looked nervously at the imposing, yellow-haired knight, but took some strength from the controlling presence at Sir Hugh's side.

'Oh, no. Though he did say he had been part of a conspiracy to kill Chimbai, and that you, Sir Hugh Leyghton, had supplied him with a weapon.'

Denials and accusations broke out across the table, drowning out David's words. Sir Hugh was red-faced with anger; in contrast Guchuluk, upon receiving de Beaujeu's translation, looked as cold as winter ice on the Thames. Falconer allowed the swell of voices to subside before waving the Nestorian priest on.

'Perhaps I did not fully understand him,' he said, placatingly. 'But he did say he felt responsible for Chimbai's death. Yes, that was the word he chose: responsible. But perhaps that was only because what he had fervently wished for had come about. I cannot now say.'

'But . . .' Sir Hugh still tried to intervene, and Falconer stayed his impatience with a firm hand on the knight's arm.

'Hear him out, Sir Hugh.'

David licked his lips, and continued. 'So, I cannot say for sure whether he did kill Chimbai or not. But it was certainly not what he wanted to confess. No, what he wanted to confess went back a lot longer than that, and had been preying on his mind for years. His meeting with our party only brought it more painfully to the fore.' David took a deep breath. 'He confessed to the sin of sodomy with a fellow Templar, Geoffrey Leyghton.'

'Nooo.' The wail that escaped Sir Hugh's mouth shocked everyone in the room into immobility. He surged from his seat, and, but for the solid oak table that stood between them, would have been at David's throat, silencing the accusation. The first to recover, Falconer grabbed a fistful of Sir Hugh's rich surcoat, and dragged him back down on to the bench. He circled his arms around the knight like bands of steel, and stared hard into his face.

'We will listen to what David has to say, Sir Hugh.'

Leyghton squirmed in Falconer's grasp, shaking his head in horrified denial. But Falconer was implacable.

'It's true, isn't it, Sir Hugh? Your brother and Bernard were discovered committing what their order called "the filthy and stinking sin that cannot be named". And he killed himself rather than be expelled from the order. He didn't die honourably at Leignitz, and you have always known that. Ever since you eavesdropped on his former comrades telling your parents of his ignominious death. You can't deny it, because Guillaume de Beaujeu was in that contingent, and knew all about your brother. He also saw you in the passageway outside the door of your parents' chamber.'

Sir Hugh crumpled over the table, trying to stop his ears like some little child refusing to hear a rebuke. When he at last looked up at his accuser, his eyes were bloodshot, and he could only manage a whisper in reply to Falconer's words: 'It's not true – Geoffrey died nobly at Leignitz. The blood-thirsty Tartars were his murderers.'

Falconer spoke more gently. 'You know in your heart that's not so. The older brother you idolized as a child let you down, didn't he? And you could not admit it. And when Bernard filled your ears with the truth the other day, you killed him for it. And cut his ear off to mutilate him as you liked to imagine your brother had been mutilated by the Tartars. It was only when I saw this as indicating a Tartar presence in the Domus that you latched on to the idea of accusing Guchuluk.'

Sir Hugh's face turned into a cold, hard mask. 'You can prove nothing. The only witness there might have been is dead.'

'Who? Bellasez – a frail, old man who you went back to kill, as soon as you had been told there was a possible witness to your murder of Bernard? I am happy to tell you that he lives, and, though still with a sore head, will be glad to point out his assailant to the constable.'

De Beaujeu now saw why Falconer had crowded Sir Hugh so close on the rigid and uncomfortable bench the friars used for their meals. Leyghton tried to rise and make a grab for the dagger at his side, but was virtually pinned down by the edge of the bench behind his knees and Falconer at his side. Still he attempted to escape, and the two men fell backwards from the bench, grappling on the floor. Falconer bellowed the constable's name at the top of his voice, and Peter Bullock burst in through the door, behind which he had no doubt been lurking all along. With Bullock's snaggle-tooth sword at his throat, Sir Hugh gave up the unequal struggle. Pulled to his feet by the constable, he shrugged the constable's rough hand off his arm, and straightened his surcoat.

'You know you have no jurisdiction over me,' he said, recovering his composure. 'I will go with you, but don't forget I am the king's ambassador. He will reject these base accusations, and it will go ill for you in the end.'

With that, he swept out of the room, followed by an uncertain constable, who shot a questioning glance at Falconer as he left. It was de Ewelme who put the constable's worry into words, whispering in Falconer's ear:

'He's right, you know. The king will see the murder of a sodomizing friar, falsely accusing Sir Hugh's brother of out-rageous conduct, as nothing more than a minor peccadillo. He will be laughing in all our faces in a few days' time.'

Falconer's expression remained calm. He chose not to reprove de Ewelme for his incorrect assumption that Bernard could both be a sodomizer of Geoffrey Leyghton and be falsely accusing him of sodomy at the same time. He stuck to what he had learned from the Templar, whose order had a network of spies at courts throughout Christendom. 'Not if de Beaujeu is to be believed. He tells me the king is not sure whether he wants to make an alliance with the Tartars or not. What he is sure of is that he wants to sit on the fence at the moment until he sees which way to leap. Sir Hugh was entrusted with keeping the matter open, something which he has signally failed to do. He even plotted to kill the Tartar ambassador, which act could have tainted Henry himself. No, I don't think Sir Hugh will find the king such a friend as he imagines.'

De Ewelme beamed in obvious relief, reassured that the reputation of the university would not be sullied in the eyes of the king.

'Then all is nicely resolved. The murder of Brother Bernard has a solution, as it would appear that Bernard himself was the murderer of the Tartar. That he met his own end because of his . . . unsavoury past is poetic justice.'

Falconer held up his hand. 'Not so fast. You heard David say that Bernard confessed to an earlier sin, but not to the murder of Chimbai.'

'But surely . . .'

De Ewelme suddenly realized that the others in the refectory were now listening to him. David had adopted his former role of translator and was whispering into the ear of Guchuluk. Though his face was as impassive as ever, the young Tartar bahadur was listening attentively, and his eyes gleamed. With a ready audience, and ever eager for the simple solution, de Ewelme pressed his case.

'This man' – he indicated David with an imperious wave of the hand – 'himself says Bernard was given a weapon by Sir Hugh, and wished to see Chimbai dead. And I understand that his Dominican brethren in this very friary saw Bernard covered in blood. What could be more conclusive?'

'The weapon Bernard was furnished with was a sword –

Geoffrey Leyghton's sword – and Chimbai died with an arrow in his chest; that does not exactly incriminate Bernard.'

'A sword? How do you know this?' stammered the discomfited chancellor.

'Because I found it where Bellasez said Bernard hid it in the Domus Conversorum. And the blood on Bernard, which he left also on the mattress of his cell, was his own. When I examined his body, there were freshly healed scars on his forearms, where he had clearly mutilated himself. No, Bernard was not the murderer we are seeking.'

'Then who is?'

Falconer frowned, and turned to address Guillaume de Beaujeu and the Tartar men assembled round the table. As Falconer spoke, David translated for Guchuluk and Yeh-Lu, though Falconer knew that the Cathay man knew every world anyway.

'I have been experiencing difficulty in establishing how Chimbai could have been killed, other than by magic. So I would like to call on the skills of a very powerful necromancer, who I took the liberty of inviting to this assembly.'

He strode over to the door, and ushered in a slight figure dressed all in grey. It was the white-haired Roger Bacon, who stood solemnly before the motley crew of Tartars, university chancellor, Templar and regent master, while the last exalted his reputation as magician and diviner of truths. Then Roger stepped forth and expounded upon those matters his astonishing mind truly believed possible, though mortal brains might marvel at this impossibility. He spoke in Latin and waved his arms theatrically in the air to further enhance his theses.

'*Nam instrumenta navigandi possunt fieri ut naves maximae ferantur uno solo homine regente, majori velocitate quam si plenae essent hominibus . . . currus possunt fieri ut sine animale moveantur cum impetu inestimabili . . . possunt fieri instrumenta volandi ut homo sedeat in medeo . . .'*

Falconer was familiar with Bacon's theories on ships driven by a single person, a wagon moving without animal power, and a flying machine. These had seemed like magic to him when Bacon had first proposed them. Now, he was sure he could make a flying machine himself. Still, he could see that everyone in the room was shaken by Bacon's assertions and was wondering where they might be leading. Finally the little friar came to the crux of his argument.

'Possunt instrumentum fieri . . . No, not *can* be made – I *have* made an instrument that can predict the course of the sun, moon and stars, and tell the hours of the day. With it, I will predict the very name of he who killed the Noyan Chimbai. I will go and set the astrarium in motion, and the answer will come at dawn tomorrow.'

The categorical prediction was accompanied by a final flourish of the hand, and Bacon bowed triumphantly out of the room.

De Beaujeu leaned across the table and hissed a disbelieving aside to Falconer:

'This is nonsense. You can't really think he is capable of this, William?'

Falconer's response was enigmatic. 'It doesn't matter what I think. It's what the killer thinks that's important. And only time will tell on that.'

Eighteen

So I hid my face from them and handed them over to their enemies, and they fell, every one of them, by the sword. I dealt with them as they deserved, defiled and rebellious as they were, and hid my face from them.

Ezekiel 39: 23—4

The old gatehouse standing at the southern end of Grandpont had seen better days. It had been built as a secure vantage point to protect the bridge; now the crumbling edifice was home to a skinner, the stink from whose trade assailed the nostrils of all those who chose to enter Oxford from the south. That he was not allowed to ply his trade inside the city walls was sufficient evidence of the scale of the rancid stink. Of course the upper room in the tower housed the altogether more acceptable pursuit of scholarship, which afforded no such assault on the nostrils.

Any nocturnal wanderer would have seen that scholarship did not keep to the regular hours pursued by the skinner and his fellow tradesmen. A candle's light flickered in the upper windows of the gatehouse tower, and, every now and then, the shadow of the tower's occupant would pass across the window arch, suggesting the man was restlessly pursuing some knotty problem. But there was no one to observe this fretful movement, as all good citizens had long retired to their beds. Even the thieving night-stalkers had abandoned the shadows, for at this late hour there was no one for them to prey on. The heavy silence was broken only by the occasional snuffle of a nocturnal creature in the nearby fields, and the insistent tinkle of the river that flowed, oblivious to the hour, past the foot of the tower, and on across Oxford's southern meadows.

Suddenly, one of the deep shadows marking the shape of a doorway close under South Gate moved and flowed quickly into the doorway next to it. Soundlessly, it flitted from doorway to doorway until it stood below the lighted window in the gatehouse tower. Lurking at the edge of the soft oblong of light cast by the candles high above, it became clear the shadow was a figure wrapped in a long, dark cloak. The head, hidden deep in the cloak's generous hood, glanced up at the window where the occupant of the room continued his restless pacing. For a moment the lower half of the person's face was caught in the yellowish rays of light, then was lost in the hood again. It was too brief a moment to identify the wearer of the cloak, even if there had been someone to observe the lapse. The figure backed away from the light and stood by the door that gave access to the broken stairs leading up to Friar Bacon's eyrie. Whoever it was blended into the darkness again, and waited patiently for his moment.

Eventually the candle was snuffed out, and the oblong of light on the ground disappeared. Again the figure waited, to allow the tower's occupant to settle into sleep, and became part of the stillness of the night that surrounded him. Finally, he tried the latch of the door. It was unbarred, and he slipped inside. The figure outlined briefly against the whitewashed wall inside the door, was holding a dark object shaped like a cooking pot in his left hand; from the way his shoulders were set, the object appeared heavy and awkward to carry.

Inside the tower he looked up at the spiral stairs – each step was heavily worn at the centre, where hundreds of feet had passed, and the rope disappearing up the left-hand wall was threadbare and unsafe. He would not trust his weight to it.

Hefting the heavy object he carried into his right hand, so that he might keep to the wider part of the stairs' tread on the left, he began his cautious ascent. Part way up, he stopped and turned his head to one side, alert to the slightest noise, like a wary, wild bird. He had thought he heard something above. Perhaps the friar had tossed in his sleep, or perhaps it was just the creak of cooling timbers in the roof . . . whatever it was had now ceased, and silence reigned. He continued his steady climb, regulating his breathing so that he did not betray his presence with an unguarded gasp for air. At the top of the stairs, the door to the turret room stood closed before him.

Still he listened hard, until he was satisfied that he had not disturbed the occupant of the room. He placed the pot he carried on the boards immediately outside the door, and carefully arranged the tallow-soaked wick that protruded from the top of the pot so that it hung over the side. The rest of the top was firmly stoppered. He stood up and removed the stub of a candle from the pocket in the sleeve of his gown. He dare not allow a spark from his flint to fall on the pot, so he would have to light the candle first, then, using the candle flame, light the wick. That should give him sufficient time to escape down the stairs before the device worked. The sound of the flint striking steel was horrifyingly loud, but it had to be endured. No other source of flame was available to him in the dead of the night. Finally, he had the candle lit and, with trembling hands, held it to the tallow-soaked wick.

The shock of the door flying open almost threw him backwards. A lantern was thrust into his face, almost blinding him.

'You were right, William,' Bacon called over his shoulder. 'It is Yeh-Lu.'

Falconer's face peered triumphantly over the friar's shoulder. 'Of course it's Yeh-Lu – only he knew about the horologium, and how he could rig it up to fire an arrow at a certain time, ensuring he himself was in our company when the fatal hour arrived. The perfect alibi: he was talking to me, the man who ended up trying to unmask the murderer, when the murder was committed – how could he possibly be the one?'

'Only by the use of a clock mechanism . . .'

'Which you told me you could use to mark the cloistral hours more precisely than a monk. Only you couldn't show it to me, because the crucial wheel that was so difficult to make was missing.'

'Stolen by Yeh-Lu.'

The two men grinned at each other with self-satisfaction, almost ignoring the prostrate form of the man from Cathay at their feet. He roared in defeated frustration, then realized the candle stub was still in his hand, and still alight. There was yet a chance. The law of getting rid of someone who has outlasted their usefulness echoed in his head: *niao chin kung ts'ang, t'u szu kou p'eng* – literally, when the rabbit has been killed, the hunting dog goes in the cooking pot. He thrust the candle flame at the wick hanging from the pot. The wick sputtered, almost died, then caught and began to burn rapidly. Falconer and Bacon looked at each other in bewilderment, while Yeh-Lu scrambled to his feet and grabbed the rope at the top of the stairs. He now had precious little time to escape before the *chen t'ien lei* – the thunder-bomb – exploded, sending flames and splinters of metal everywhere.

Falconer grabbed at Yeh-Lu's heavy cloak, and called out to Bacon to extinguish the wick. Whatever was in the pot, he knew it was not going to be pleasant when the flames got to it. Bacon bent over the pot, flapping at the wick, inadvertently sending sparks everywhere, including into the opening at the top of the pot. Yeh-Lu's eyes opened wide in horror, and he tore himself from Falconer's grasp. He took a few lurching steps down the stairs before losing his balance. He grabbed at the rope that spiralled down the wall and for a moment he held it, almost pulling himself upright. Then the rotten rope parted just above his clutching fingers, and, with an awful cry, he tumbled down the stairs and out of Falconer's view.

Falconer heard a fizzing sound behind him, and turned to see Bacon staring bemusedly into the pot from which unearthly green sputtering flames emanated. The friar's white hair was singed right across his blackened forehead, but there was a smile on his face.

'He must have got the mixture wrong – saltpetre, sulphur and charcoal . . . notoriously difficult to get right. Did you know the Arabs call saltpetre Chinese Snow?'

Falconer found Yeh-Lu at the foot of the perilous spiral steps with his head twisted at an impossible angle. His neck had been broken. Bacon expressed some feelings of sorrow at this fatal conclusion to Falconer's murder hunt. The man from Cathay had been an engineer of some brilliance, with a repository of knowledge handed down from his Peking ancestors. His chief expertise had been in the construction of clocks, which Su Sung had invented a hundred years earlier. Unfortunately this knowledge had been of little interest to the Tartars who had overrun Cathay as brutally as they had the eastern part of Christendom. They were more interested in the military inventions of the Peking scientists, which included explosive powder, incendiaries and smoke bombs.

'I spoke with Yeh-Lu about clocks on the road to Oxford. He feigned only a polite interest at first, but when I gave him some mathematical details about a pinion of twelve carrying a wheel of twenty teeth meshing with a wheel of twenty four on the great wheel, he could see that I knew what I was talking about. Then we spoke together as fellow scientists. I even told him I had the makings of a clock in my baggage.'

'And you showed him the clock when you set it up in this room?'

Bacon nodded his head sadly. 'Yes. He was here once when you came round. He had extracted a promise from me that I would tell no one of his visits, so I had to get rid of you. My apologies for so upsetting you. Then he rewarded me by stealing the central mechanism – in order to use it for an automatic device to kill Chimbai.'

'How did you work out it was Yeh-Lu, and not Guchuluk or David, who killed Chimbai?'

Guillaume de Beaujeu was walking the ramparts of the city with Falconer the day after Yeh-Lu's body had been returned to the Tartars. Neither man knew what Guchuluk would do with the corpse, but that was a matter for the Tartar bahadur. Although the consequences of Yeh-Lu's act would no doubt be felt far away in remotest Karakorum, it would cause scarcely a ripple in the placid atmosphere of Oxford. Scholar and Templar watched as the Tartar soldiers began to strike their camp and the strange circular tents were stripped to skeletal ribs of wood. Then even this framework was pulled down, leaving only a pale circular patch on the grass, which would itself disappear within a few days. Ironically, the Tartars had come and would soon be gone without any great effect on the lives lived by Falconer and his fellows – a passing curiosity as ephemeral as the elephant that had preceded them.

Falconer's reply to de Beaujeu's question was teasing; 'Or you, Sir Hugh Leyghton, or Bernard de Genova, for that matter.'

The Templar knew it was unlikely to have been one of these. He felt the two letters that were stuffed inside his jerkin, one of which commanded a member of Chimbai's entourage to kill him. He now knew it had been intended for Yeh-Lu, and to have shown it to Falconer straight away would have simplified the scholar's investigations considerably. But he had been under instructions to keep the letter secret, and in the end Falconer, as clever as ever, had worked it out for himself. He listened politely as Falconer concluded his exposition.

'I was diverted for a long while by the seeming impossibility of Chimbai's death. How could a man be killed by an arrow in an otherwise empty tent? I wasted a lot of time assuming the arrow had been fired from outside. But that proved impossible, too. I had been told by Guchuluk at the beginning how Chimbai's body lay in the tent, but it took me some time to see what that fact told me: if Chimbai lay face up, with his head towards the tent opening, and the arrow in his chest, he could not have been killed from outside. The arrow must have started and ended its journey inside the tent. It was only when someone spoke to me about wishing to be in two places at once – ' for a moment Falconer's thoughts lingered on Ann Segrim and her sweet form – 'that I realized how useful that would be for a murderer. If the murderer could kill – or at least arrange the killing – and be somewhere else when it happened, his innocence would be evident. Without a human agent to be found and broken, the murderer was safe. Until I asked to look inside the tent. You see, Yeh-Lu had not had a chance to remove the clock mechanism, and he knew that if I saw it, I would understand its significance. So he set fire to the tent to burn the evidence.'

'But why suspect Yeh-Lu specifically?'

'Because he was the only one who had gone out of his way to set up witnesses to prove where he was when Chimbai stood in front of his gods and was killed. He chose me and

Roger Bacon, because we had no connection with Chimbai, and no reason to be suspected of his death ourselves. I knew it was Yeh-Lu then, and his knowledge of both clocks and Chimbai's morning routine only confirmed my suspicions. My little subterfuge at the meeting I asked you to call – Roger's extravagant claims for his astrarium – was simply to get him to reveal himself to us. To either of the other Tartars, the pronouncement would be just what Roger claimed it to be: a magical prophecy. Only Yeh-Lu would know that Roger's mad claim carried a veiled threat to reveal the truth – that Roger knew what he had done – and would draw him into trying to obliterate that truth.'

'You used Bacon like Tartar suicide troops fleeing from the enemy, only to draw them into a deadly trap.'

'The *mangudai* manœuvre. Except the suicide troops – both Bacon and myself actually – nearly got blown up in the process!'

Falconer's final words were accompanied by a doleful toll of a distant bell. They waited for it to cease, but it continued with a demented persistence. The truth then dawned on Falconer: Roger had at last got his horologium to mark the hours, but he had failed to work out how to get the device to cease. The peal of the bell was joined by the two men's peals of laughter.

Epilogue

I will show my glory amongst the nations; all shall see the judgement that I execute and the heavy hand that I lay upon them.

Ezekiel 39:21

The only man eventually prepared to trust the Mongols was Prince Edward, son and heir to King Henry, when he reached the Holy Land in 1271. There he met a like mind in Tedaldo Visconti (who was to be Pope Gregory X), who himself then encountered two Venetian merchants called Niccolò and Maffeo Polo, fresh from their travels to Kublay's fabled court. Mongol ambassadors addressed the Fourteenth Ecumenical Council at Lyons in 1274, and came to England to meet Edward, by then king. It all came to nothing – the only member of Gregory's embassy to reach China for the first time was Niccolo Polo's seventeen-year-old-son, Marco. There is a passing reference in Marco Polo's accounts of his travels to a member of the royal household called Guchuluk. It may not be the same man who came to England and met William Falconer – the name is a common one.

Around the time of the Council of Lyons Guillaume de Beaujeu became the Grand Master of the Order of the Poor Knights of the Temple. He served in that capacity nobly and well, refraining from most of the devious excesses of his predecessors. It was fortunate he did not live to see the end of the Templars. The order was to survive for only another thirty years before the bitter enmity of the French king brought about its downfall.

Nicholas de Ewelme had an undistinguished career as chancellor of the University of Oxford, remaining stubbornly ambitious without evincing any of the skills in diplomacy that the post required. He was removed within two years of appointment, and was succeeded by Thomas Bek.

Peter Bullock died a warrior's death, much to his own surprise, having thought he would die like an old man, in bed. He accidentally found himself in the way of a rusty sword swung by a Welsh student in the midst of a pitched battle between northern and Welsh clerks. He bled to death in the dusty street, pondering on the ironies of a Welshman bringing about his downfall. His sister had married a man called Owain, whom he had had no time for.

William Falconer was to have many further murder puzzles to unravel, and, curiously, appears in a footnote to the records of the Chancellor's Court, accused of murder himself. The result of the trial is not recorded, but it is said Falconer left Oxford later in life to travel to Cathay in search of Peking engineers and information about flight.